Game Plan

A Brooklyn Monarchs novella/Book 4

Patricia Sargeant (aka Regina Hart)

Game Plan

A Brooklyn Monarchs novella/Book 4

By Patricia Sargeant (aka Regina Hart)

Published by Mediopolis Communications, LLC

Cover designer: Michael A. Matthews

Interior layout: Formatting Fairies

ISBN-10: 0-9985366-1-X

ISBN-13: 978-0-9985366-1-3

www.PatriciaSargeant.com

Please go to my website, PatriciaSargeant.com, to sign up for my enewsletter for the latest on my upcoming releases, events and giveaways.

Game Plan *is the fourth book in the Brooklyn Monarchs contemporary sports romance series, which features the fictitious professional basketball franchise. This fourth story, a novella, focuses on two couples: Anthony "The Saint" Chambers and Faith Wilcox, and Serge Gateau and Constance Street.*

If you want to win the game, you have to have a plan. . .

NBA hooper and self-proclaimed Bible scholar Anthony "The Saint" Chambers finally earned his championship ring after his Brooklyn Monarchs crowned their Cinderella season. Now in the offseason, Anthony is planning the next move in his career – more money, fame and game – as the Monarchs lace up to defend their title. But falling in love wasn't part of the plan ...

Struggling artist Faith Chambers is an administrative assistant by day and a promising cartoonist by night. Her plans include publishing contracts, television agreements and paying her rent on time. Yet she risks all of that for a Bible-quoting baller. When Faith's finances get even sketchier, Anthony's teammates paint a dubious picture of her real intent. Is Faith drawn to Anthony – or his money? Will Faith and Anthony's relationship be sidelined by suspicion or will they stick to their original game plan and fall in love?

Game Plan
A Brooklyn Monarchs novella/Book 4

"I want to apologize." Anthony raised his voice so Faith could hear him over the celebratory sounds of Constance's birthday party.

"What are you apologizing for?" Faith's chocolate gaze was direct and inescapable.

Anthony stepped closer so he didn't have to shout. Beneath the scents of confectioner's sugar and warm hors d'oeuvres, he caught a hint of Faith's citrus and rose perfume. "I think you know what I'm apologizing for."

"I know what you *should* be apologizing for, but why are you actually apologizing?" Her voice carried the barest trace of sinful Southern nights. He could almost smell the magnolias.

"Why are we playing guessing games?"

"I thought you were apologizing."

"I'm trying to."

"Who put you up to this apology, Troy or Serge?"

"Both." He wasn't going to lie. "But you shouldn't withhold forgiveness just because I didn't initially realize it on my own."

"You're right. 'For if ye forgive men their trespasses, your heavenly Father will also forgive you.'"

"Matthew six fourteen." Anthony looked at her with new eyes. "You know your bible."

"You haven't cornered the market on sanctimony, Saint Anthony." She addressed him by the hated nickname that his teammate had given him.

If he corrected her, he had a feeling, she'd ignore him. "Then why won't you accept my apology?"

Dedication

To my dream team:

- *My sister, Bernadette, for giving me the dream*
- *My husband, Michael, for supporting the dream*
- *My brother Richard for believing in the dream*
- *My brother Gideon for encouraging the dream*

And to Mom and Dad always with love.

Thank you to all the readers who encouraged me to continue the Brooklyn Monarchs' professional basketball journey. I hope you enjoy their new season.

Chapter 1

"Groupies aren't allowed on the practice court." The irritated male voice came out of nowhere, echoing around the indoor basketball court. Faith Wilcox's heart almost stopped.

She bobbled the cellular phone she'd been using to take a selfie of herself standing over the Brooklyn Monarchs logo painted onto the center of the National Basketball Association franchise's practice court. Faith regained possession of the device before it bounced onto the hardwood and shattered at her feet. She dropped it into her oversized lavender tote bag, which swung from her right shoulder.

Whew!

Faith turned toward the voice. Her flirty pastel patterned skirt swung around her knees. It was late in the afternoon of the last Saturday in August. The lighting in the practice facility was bright, bouncing off the pale silver walls.

Anthony "The Saint" Chambers stood scowling at her near the entrance to the locker rooms. She knew a lot about Brooklyn, New York's NBA team, including its roster. One of her roommates worked for the Monarchs and the other had been a sports reporter assigned to the team for years.

Good Lord, the man was tall!

Watching the players' interviews on television didn't prepare her for this up-close-and-personal encounter. Faith tugged her eyes from his broad, well-sculpted chest wrapped in a tight silver T-shirt and raised it to his face. His disgruntled scowl didn't detract one bit from his cover model good looks: almond-shaped olive eyes that were startling against golden skin; blade-like cheekbones; and a spare, squared jaw. His full, well-shaped lips kept his features from crossing the line into cold and hard.

His words finally registered. *Does he think I'm a* groupie*?*

Faith found her voice. "I'm waiting for Serge Gateau."

Serge was the six-foot-ten Monarchs forward. The blue-eyed blonde Frenchman also was a friend.

A knowing gleam formed in The Saint's eyes. He gave her a dismissive look as he adjusted the silver and black nylon gym bag on his left shoulder. "I'm sorry, sweetheart, Serge is spoken for."

Sweetheart? Oh, no. I am not *the one.* "My name isn't sweetheart. It's Faith."

"I'm sorry, Faith, but you have to leave. It's policy." He jerked his Michael Ealy-like jawline in the direction of the exit behind her.

"You're not listening to me." Which was ironic, considering the practice court magnified their voices. A calming breath drew in the faint scent of sweat and the lemon floor wax from the high-gloss court. "I'm not leaving. I'm waiting for Serge. He's a friend."

Anthony lowered the two thick slashes that were his eyebrows. His good looks were a distraction. They almost made up for his rudeness. Almost.

"Sure he is." Anthony braced his long legs in his knee-length khaki shorts. "I doubt his lady would want you within fifty yards of him. Do you need me to escort you out?"

Faith's rising temper chased away the slight chill in the facility. She wasn't some criminal to be escorted from the court. Why wouldn't this blockhead believe her?

She jabbed a finger at the hardwood court and pinned the gorgeous grump with a stormy stare. "Troy asked me to wait right here while he got Serge. So if my presence offends you, *you* can leave."

"Troy Marshall?" Anthony's expression blanked with surprise and confusion.

Ah, Mr. Know-It-All wasn't ready for that. "Do you know another Troy?"

Troy was the Brooklyn Monarchs vice president of media and marketing. And a friend.

"How do *you* know him?"

Was he another one of those cute guys who didn't have two common sense cells to rub together? How disappointing.

"I'm done talking." Faith checked her bright gold timepiece. An image of Tinker Bell, the feisty fairy from J.M. Barrie's Peter Pan play, soared across the center of the watch's face in beautiful technicolor.

What was taking Troy and Serge so long?

The Saint was working Faith's last fragile nerve. She just wanted to give Serge the information she'd promised him and leave.

When she glanced up, Anthony was still staring at her. "What?"

"Who are you?"

"I told you."

The doors to the locker room opened behind Anthony. Serge appeared, followed by Troy. Like Anthony, Serge wore a dark

T-shirt and knee-length shorts. Troy stood out in his three-button navy Italian suit and black Italian leather shoes.

"Faith!" Serge gave her his heartthrob smile, the one that made his dark blue eyes twinkle like sapphires and deepened the dimple in his left cheek.

"Hi, Serge." At the sight of her friend's boyfriend, Faith felt a wave of both pleasure and relief.

Serge circled Anthony to pull Faith into a bear hug. "Sorry to keep you waiting."

"I know you can't rush perfection." Faith stepped back with a grin. Her gaze moved between Serge and Troy. "Why are you at the practice facility a month early? Training camp doesn't start until the end of September."

Serge's blonde eyebrows rose in surprise. "You've been bulking up on your basketball knowledge."

Faith's cheeks heated. "It's self-defense since both of my roommates are dating Monarchs men."

"We're here early because we have a championship to defend." Serge glanced over his shoulder, his smile still in place. "I see you've met Saint Anthony."

"Yes, I did." Faith heard the coolness in her voice. She smiled at Troy. "Thank you for allowing me to wait here for Serge."

"Of course." The Monarchs executive seemed puzzled by her words.

With his smooth sienna skin, rich curly black hair, mustache and goatee, and swoon-worthy coal black eyes, Troy looked more like a model or film star than a business executive. He also looked like he could have played professional ball, but he hadn't. The media executive was dating her roommate Andrea Benson, a newspaper reporter. Constance Street, Faith's other roommate and Troy's administrative assistant, was dating Serge. They were both lucky.

Faith shot a look toward Anthony. *Why is he still here?* She did her best to ignore him and instead focused on Serge and Troy.

"Last-minute instructions." Faith took two sheets of printer paper from her tote bag. She folded the first and gave it to Serge. "This sheet lists Connie's sizes – shoes, pants, blouses and sexy things." She winked at him, then turned the second sheet so they could read it together. "Andrea and I think Connie would want these friends to attend. We've got that covered. This column lists Connie's and Tiff's favorite foods. Andrea and I will bring those dishes to the party." Tiffany was Constance's three-year-old daughter.

"What're you talking about?" Anthony's question interrupted Faith's instructions.

Serge's excitement was palpable - and adorable. "This is for the surprise birthday party we're planning for Connie. You sent your reply."

Comprehension eased Anthony's expression. "I got the invitation a couple of weeks ago. Thanks."

Faith frowned at him. "You're coming?"

Anthony nodded. "Yes."

Oh. Joy.

She turned back to Serge. "Let Andrea and me know if you need help with anything."

"You've already done so much. Thank you." Serge squeezed her shoulder.

"We're in this together." Faith adjusted her tote bag on her shoulder, and smiled at Troy and Serge. "Remember, mum's the word." She nodded to Anthony, then turned to leave.

Serge had invited all of his teammates and several people from the Monarchs' front office to Constance's surprise birthday party. It shouldn't surprise her that he'd invited St. Obnoxious. A line from Psalm 23 came to her. "Thou preparest a table for me in the midst of mine enemies." She'd just have to avoid him. In a crowd of fifty or more people, how hard would that be?

***

I'm an idiot.

Anthony watched Faith walk away. Her strappy, yellow sandals tapped across the hardwood court, keeping time with his pulse. In her pale pink sleeveless blouse and flirty knee-length peach and white skirt, she looked like a spring day.

He'd been shocked into motionless silence when Serge had wrapped her in a bear hug like a brother who hadn't seen his sister in months. Troy also was fond of her. Anthony could still taste his foot in his mouth.

"What did you do?"

Anthony turned to Serge. Could he play it off? "What d'you mean?"

Serge's French accent deepened. "Why did one of the nicest people I've ever known give you the cold shoulder?"

"I was wondering the same thing." Troy's piercing coal black eyes dragged Anthony back to bible camp and his fear of spontaneous confessions.

Anthony couldn't blame the two men for ganging up on him. He was shamed by his behavior toward a woman who'd been telling the truth.

"I didn't know who she was so I asked her to leave." The defensive tone of his voice made him wince.

Troy recovered first, swinging an arm toward the doors. "How do you think she'd gotten past security?"

"I didn't consider that." And now he felt even smaller.

"What did she say when you asked her to leave?" Irritation tightened Serge's voice.

It kept getting worse. "She told me Troy had brought her here to wait for you. I didn't believe her."

Visibly dumbstruck, Serge looked from Anthony to Troy, then back. "Why not?"

Good question.

He'd been in junior high school the last time a female had taken him out of his comfort zone. Was it the way she'd looked at him with such blatant appreciation? Or the way she'd stood up to him when he'd told her to leave? Both potential explanations were ridiculous – but Serge and Troy were waiting for an answer.

"I thought she was a groupie." Anthony muttered the words as he massaged the knotted muscles in the back of his neck.

Troy shook his head. "How could you have acted so stupidly?"

"*Very* stupidly and I'm certain you offended Faith." In his irritation, Serge's French accent was even more pronounced.

Anthony wished he could go back in time and shake some sense into himself. "I'm very sorry."

"Apologize to Faith." Troy's words were a demand.

Anthony's eyes widened. "I don't think that would go over well. She's pretty angry."

"She has a right to be." Serge drew himself to his full height, which was three inches over Anthony.

"We don't care how you think it'll go over." Troy's voice was firm. "You owe Faith an apology."

"You're right." Anthony checked his silver Movado wristwatch. "Look, I've got someplace to be, but I promise I'll apologize to Faith."

Both men looked satisfied. Anthony turned to leave.

Apologizing to Faith was the right thing to do, but based on the chill she'd left behind, it would be harder than earning back-to-back NBA titles. Would he be able to find the right words to ask for her forgiveness? Maybe he should remind her of Matthew chapter six, verse fourteen, "For if you forgive others their trespasses, your heavenly Father will also forgive you."

***

Later that afternoon, Anthony leaned forward on his older brother's blue and green plaid fabric sofa. He ran his right index and middle fingers over the edge of the walnut coffee table. The tips of both digits came back covered in dust.

Anthony held up his right hand to his brother. "Paul, have you ever thought about running a duster over your stuff, man?"

Paul Chambers, ten years Anthony's senior, grunted from his slouched position at the far end of the sofa. He wore his standard uniform of dark oversized T-shirt and matching warm-up pants. "You gonna hire someone to do that shit for me?"

"This isn't the way Mom raised us." Anthony cut off the rest of his response, which included pointing out that he'd made the down payment on his brother's two-bedroom/two-and-a-half bath condominium in the prosperous Prospect Heights neighborhood of Brooklyn, New York. Why should he also foot the bill for regular – and extensive - cleaning services, something Paul could either pay for or do himself?

Anthony looked around the room, ignoring the sneakers and various articles of clothing strewn here and there. The simple coffee table and jarring sofa with its matching armchair didn't feel like enough furniture for the large living room. The pieces were assembled in an almost worshipful formation in front of the huge black flat screen television. The gray wall-to-wall carpeting was out of place.

"Dusting?" Paul frowned. "You're gonna hassle me about dusting? Man, I already have too much else shit to do, running your foundation."

That's the other thing Anthony had bitten back. He'd paid for the college education that had given his brother his undergraduate degree in finance and his master's degree in business administration. He'd also started the Florence Chambers Foundation in honor of their deceased mother and created the director's position for Paul. He loved his brother and he owed him a lot. Helping him was his pleasure not a burden, but some things Paul could do own his own – like cleaning.

"Fine, that's not what you asked me here for anyway." Anthony shifted on the sofa to face his brother. "What did you want to talk about?"

Paul was almost a mirror image to him. Same olive eyes. Same pale brown skin. About the same height. His features were rounder, though. Paul had at least twenty pounds on him.

"Your Monarchs contract."

That response took Anthony by surprise. "What about it?"

"You need more money."

He could feel his stomach muscles tighten and twist. This wasn't the first time his older brother had complained about the terms of Anthony's contract. Even if the day came that he made top dollar, he'd bet his bonuses that Paul would still say it wasn't enough.

"I'll worry about that when it's time to renegotiate." Anthony injected a note of finality into his response. Hopefully, Paul would take the hint and drop the subject.

He didn't. "The time's now."

"I still have this season left on my contract. I can't renegotiate now."

"Man, people do it all the time."

"How do you know?" Anthony tried to hide his impatience.

His brother wasn't in the NBA. The only people Paul knew who were associated with the league were Anthony and Anthony's agent, so how did he get to name himself an expert on NBA contracts?

"I hear about it on the news all the time." Paul shrugged his shoulders beneath his dark gray T-shirt. A corporate brand logo appeared on the center of his chest above the curvature of his belly.

"You can't believe everything you see or read in the media." Anthony's teammate, shooting guard Warrick Evans, and his wife, Dr. Marilyn DeVry-Evans, had learned that the hard way.

Restless, Anthony crossed to the fireplace. The mantel was crowded with photographs and trophies of Paul's success as a high school basketball player. He'd been the star of the team and a standout in the region. Paul had had dreams of playing in the NBA and having his own line of sneakers.

Then their father had died of a massive coronary. Paul had quit his high school team and gotten a job to help support the family. When then-six-year-old Anthony had shown an interest in Paul's game, he'd inherited brother's dreams.

Paul came to stand beside him at the mantel. "You're a champion now, Tony. You need to stop thinking like a chump." Paul planted the index and middle fingers of his right hand against Anthony's hairline and shoved his head back.

Why did Paul always make his arguments physical? That head-shoving maneuver had been annoying when Anthony was a boy. Now that they were both men, he found the tactic even more aggravating.

Anthony scowled at him before crossing to the double windows on the far side of the living room. From Paul's thirteenth floor condo, Anthony let the summer-in-the-city scene playing out on the streets below help put the brakes on his irritation. Couples and families with and without pets had meandered out to enjoy the late afternoon's cooling temperatures.

Joggers wound their way through the neighborhood toward nearby Prospect Park. An army of farmers market vendors were set up for their Saturday sales a couple of streets away. Would this latest argument with Paul end in time for him to purchase fresh produce before the farmers packed up for the day?

"The franchise is still struggling financially." He spoke with his back to his older brother. "But by the time my contract is up at the end of this season, it should be in a better position to give me what I want."

Two of the Monarchs' three owners, Albert Tipton and Gerald Bimm, had brought the franchise to the brink of bankruptcy. By the time Jaclyn Jones, the third owner, had asserted herself, the franchise was hemorrhaging money and on the verge of being tossed out of its home court, the Empire Arena. It had taken Jaclyn's strength of will; the determination of their rookie head coach, DeMarcus Guinn; and a ton of unprecedented teamwork on the part of the players to save the Monarchs from themselves.

"I could care less about Jackie Jones's money problems. *You* need to be paid *now*." Paul's impatience hammered at Anthony from across the room. "You need to play for a team that makes *you* the star and *pays* you like one."

Anthony turned away from the window. "I want to play for the Monarchs. They're my home team and I'm happy here."

"You're *happy*? *Happy*?" Paul strode toward him. "You know you wouldn't be where you are without me, right?"

"Yeah, Paul, I know." *And you keep reminding me.* Anthony stepped back. He didn't want this argument with his brother, nor did he want Paul to shove his head again.

"You know what would make you *happy*? More money. Bet."

It was time to go. Anthony turned toward the door. "Maybe that would make *you* happy, Paul, but this isn't about you."

Since their mother had died several years ago, they were all the family they had left. He didn't want to disappoint Paul, but he didn't want to disappoint himself, either. Why did it have to be one or the other? What would it take to convince Paul that he could make his own decisions regarding his career?

Chapter 2

"I want to apologize." The following Saturday afternoon, Anthony raised his voice so Faith could hear him over the celebratory sounds of Constance's birthday party.

Their guest of honor had been completely surprised. Constance's reaction was both sweet and comical. Right now, the littlest hostess, Tiffany, was accompanying Constance and Serge around Serge's Prospect Heights condo to thank their guests for coming.

"What are you apologizing for?" Faith's chocolate gaze was direct and inescapable.

Anthony stepped closer so he didn't have to shout. Beneath the scents of confectioner's sugar and warm hors d'oeuvres, he caught a hint of Faith's citrus and rose perfume. "I think you know what I'm apologizing for."

"I know what you *should* be apologizing for, but why are you actually apologizing?" Her voice carried the barest trace of sinful Southern nights. He could almost smell the magnolias.

At six-foot-seven-inches, Anthony was almost a foot taller than her, even in those silly three-inch heels she wore.

Then why do I feel as though she's looking down on me?

In his mind, Anthony had envisioned this encounter going in a very different way. He'd approached Faith and offered his apology. *I want to apologize. No hard feelings, right?*

She'd accepted his apology. *Of course not. It was a simple misunderstanding.*

Then they'd go their separate ways. Never had he considered that she'd challenge him. What did she expect him to say? Anthony looked away. He needed to clear his mind.

Serge, Faith, Andrea and even Tiffany had spent a lot of time and care on Constance's party. Balloons, streamers and confetti in a variety of vibrant colors, and featuring various comic strip characters accented the living and dining rooms. Tiffany must have been in charge of the decorations.

Both rooms were packed with friends Constance had made at work with the Monarchs and through volunteering with the Morning Glory Chapel's homeless shelter. Many of the revelers had come with spouses and children. That explained the child-friendly menu, music and beverages. Based on conversations with his teammates, some guests, including him, also had brought gifts for Constance's daughter.

Anthony spotted Serge and Constance in conversation with a teammate who'd come with his wife and son. The Monarchs forward had balanced Tiffany in the crook of one arm and had wrapped Constance with the other. The trio looked right together: the blue-eyed blonde giant with his green-eyed, blonde princesses.

The pinch in his chest felt like envy. He shook it off and turned back to Faith. "Why are we playing guessing games?"

She arched a saucy black eyebrow. "I thought you were apologizing."

"I'm trying to."

Faith was a lovely woman with a tough demeanor. Her full pink lips formed a cupid's bow. A wealth of wavy dark brown hair framed her softly rounded honey gold face. Her purple knee-length, sleeveless dress hugged her willowy figure and exposed her slender well-toned arms.

When he'd first entered Serge's condo before everyone had gathered to surprise Constance, he'd seen Faith. She'd smiled as she welcomed other guests, and her smile had stolen his breath. He needed to see that smile again.

"Who put you up to this apology, Troy or Serge?" Faith's question brought Anthony back to the present.

"Both." He wasn't going to lie. "But you shouldn't withhold forgiveness just because I didn't initially realize it on my own."

"You're right. 'For if ye forgive men their trespasses, your heavenly Father will also forgive you.'"

"Matthew six fourteen." That was the passage he'd planned to say to her. Anthony looked at her with new eyes. "You know your bible."

"You haven't cornered the market on sanctimony, Saint Anthony." She addressed him by the hated nickname that his teammate, Monarchs center Vincent Jardine, had given him.

If he corrected her, he had a feeling, she'd ignore him. "Then why won't you accept my apology?"

"You don't understand what you're apologizing for." Her softly accented voice was tight with indignation. "You looked at me, made assumptions based on heaven knows what, then dismissed me. You know, the good book also says, 'Judge not, that ye be not judged.' Matthew seven, verse three." Faith gave him her back and stalked away.

She was right. He *had* judged her without knowing her. That was thoughtless and cruel. If someone had done that to him, he also would have found it hard to forgive. *So how could I have done that to someone else?* His rudeness had been an injustice to her. He'd also hurt himself.

Watching Faith put distance between them, Anthony was ashamed. He wanted to make it up to her. He wanted to make it up to himself. Most of all, he wanted to get to know this assertive, bible-quoting woman. Would she give him one more chance to apologize? He'd have to work harder on his next one. It would probably be his last.

***

Tuesday evening, the telephone starting ringing as soon as Constance crossed into the apartment she shared with Faith, Andrea and Tiffany. She shepherded Tiffany farther into their home. Most likely, the caller was a telemarketer. Friends, family and important contacts had each woman's individual cell phone number.

Constance hurried to answer the summons anyway. "Hello?"

"Where've you been? I've been callin' all day." The aggrieved voice on the other end of the line reminded Constance of one other person who didn't have her personal number: her mother.

"I just got in from work. Can this wait?" Constance released Tiffany's small, warm hand and watched her daughter race into their shared bedroom, a flash of hot pink and navy blue. The outfit was a birthday present from Faith for Tiffany.

"No, it cannot." Bettie Lee Maddox breathed a martyr's sigh. "Didn't you hear what I just said? I've been callin' *all day* and I won't wait a minute longer."

Constance glanced at the cold, silver cordless receiver in her hand. The message indicator light wasn't on. She put the instrument to her ear again. "We don't have any messages."

"I didn't leave any." The response was sharp with impatience. "Give me your phone number at work."

Constance's heart almost stopped. "I can't."

"Why not?"

I don't want you calling me at work. Ever. Truth be told, Constance wasn't real keen on listening to her mother now. If she could turn back time, she'd have let the darn phone ring.

"My employer doesn't want us taking personal calls at work." It was a cowardly lie but it would prevent an endless argument.

"Well, that's just stupid. Give me your cell phone number."

"I don't have one." This lie would save her sanity.

Tiffany reappeared, holding aloft another outfit she'd received as a gift during Constance's party three days prior. "Mama, help me dress?"

It was a silver Monarchs T-shirt and black exercise shorts in the smallest size imaginable. She loved it – and so did Tiffany. Constance forced a smile and allowed her baby to lead her into their bedroom. Tiffany's hand felt warm and trusting in hers.

"Jeez, Connie, everybody's got a cell phone."

"I need to get Tiff's dinner. Is there something I can help you with?"

"Why didn't you tell me about your new boyfriend?" Bettie Lee's voice became coy.

Dread washed over Constance like dirty river water. "What are you talking about?"

"That basketball player you've been datin', Serge Ghetto." A pause. "He isn't *black*, is he?"

Constance closed her eyes and breathed deeply to ease the sinking feeling in her gut. "No, Mother, he isn't black."

But black, white, yellow, red, purple or green, rich or poor, Serge Gateau was eons better than Wade Street had ever been even on the only best day of his life, which apparently, Constance and Tiffany had missed.

Constance sank onto the side of the lumpy, full-sized bed she shared with her daughter, the only good thing Wade had given her during their horrible three-year marriage. She balanced the now warm telephone receiver between her cheek and shoulder to free her hands. With a parent's skillful flexibility, she continued her odious conversation with her mother while she helped her daughter change into her new play outfit. They took the little sneakers off first.

"Why did I have to find out about Serge from Wade?" Her mother slipped back into her default grumpy voice. In the background, Constance heard gunshots, screams and explosions. Bettie Lee was watching her cable television programs again. The least she could do was turn down the volume.

"You still keep in touch with Wade?" Constance wasn't surprised. Bettie Lee had always liked her estranged husband. That's why her mother had encouraged her to marry him. That's why she'd pressured Constance to stay married to him, even when his temper had sent her to the emergency room.

Constance helped Tiffany pull off her blouse and slip off her jeans. She watched as the little girl placed her sneakers in the closet and took her clothes to the laundry hamper in the corner. May she always be so neat and well-organized.

"Wade's family." Bettie Lee's voice hardened. "You may have filed for your fancy divorce, but in the eyes of God, you'll always be married to him."

God wouldn't be that cruel. "Once the divorce is final, he'll be out of Tiff's and my life. That's what matters."

Constance heard the faint sound of metal scrapping against plastic. Her mother had finished her microwave dinner.

She helped Tiffany put on her baggy exercise shorts and Monarchs T-shirt. Her daughter rewarded her with a brilliant smile that healed her heart before the little girl raced back out of the bedroom, a flash of silver and black.

Bettie Lee burped. "Wade told me you were leavin' him because of this wealthy basketball player."

Constance's temper started a slow burn. "I left Wade because he beat me and hit my daughter."

Bettie Lee's grunt was the extent of her caring. "Well, when you marry this rich basketball player, you make sure to move me into your new home's mother-in-law suite. I can't be cramped up in this hovel while you're livin' in the lap of luxury up there in New York."

"Who said we're getting married?"

"Isn't that why you're sleepin' with him?"

Constance counted to ten while she searched for her patience. "I'm not sleeping with him, and I don't appreciate your making assumptions about my life."

"You were always so priggish. No one could stand to be around you."

"You know, Mother, I was hoping you'd called to wish me a belated happy birthday. Yesterday was the actual day." In addition to being her birthday, yesterday also had been Labor Day and Constance had had the whole day off. Her mother hadn't called, though. But Constance hadn't been surprised. This wasn't the first birthday Bettie Lee had missed.

"You know I can't remember birthdays." Bettie Lee muttered the lame excuse. Funny, she always remembered Wade's.

"You were there for my birth, Mother. I'm the only child you have."

Bettie Lee gasped. "You've gotten awfully lippy."

Faith and Andrea must be rubbing off on her. Imagine what her mother would think if she knew she and Tiffany were living with two black women.

Constance rose from the bed. "I need to go. I have to fix Tiff's dinner. She's doing well, thriving in her new home, in case you wondered."

"Talk to Serge about that mother-in-law suite. Make him understand that, when you get married, you'll need certain provisions for family."

Constance clenched her left hand at her side. "No, Mother, I'm not going to do that. Tiff and I are building a life for ourselves. You'll have to look after your own needs." As you always have.

She disconnected the call in the middle of her mother's outraged rant.

Constance stood, staring blindly at the wall on the other side of the tiny room. No, this wasn't payback for all the times she'd gone to her mother, bloodied and broken after one of Wade's beatings only to be sent home. This was about taking a stand for a positive, confident, loving future for her and her daughter. She considered the cordless phone clenched in her fist. Constance hoped Serge would want to be a part of that future, and she'd do whatever she could to keep Bettie Lee in her past.

CHAPTER 3

Anthony was dripping sweat as he let himself into his two-thousand-square-foot condominium in his Prospect Heights neighborhood Wednesday morning. His cell phone started ringing as soon as he locked his front door behind him, almost as though the caller knew he'd arrived home.

He dug the device from the Velcro pocket of his baggy navy jogging shorts. The screen displayed his agent's personal cell phone number. What was so important that it couldn't wait until Nyles Todd got to his office?

"Nyles, what's up?" Anthony was breathing hard.

"Tony, how's it goin', my man?" His agent of less than a year was still trying to decide whether they were friends or business partners. Anthony had already decided: They weren't friends.

"I'm fine. I'm on the clock, though." Anthony grabbed a glass from the blonde wood cabinet above his sink. He filled it with filtered water from his silver faucet, then drained it.

He checked his black sports watch. It was minutes after eight in the morning. He wanted to get cleaned up, then stop by Faith's workplace. Serge had given him the name of the accounting firm she worked for and he'd found the address on the internet. Hopefully, she'll accept his second attempt at an apology. Then he could arrive at the Monarchs' practice facility with a clear conscience to reassure Serge and Troy that he'd reconciled with their friend.

"Oh, sure, sure, Saint." The tinny sound on the other end of the telephone line reminded Anthony of a microwave timer. Nyles must be making his breakfast as they spoke.

Anthony bit back a sigh. "I've already told you that I hate that nickname."

One of the many reasons he missed his previous agent, God rest his soul, was that the seasoned professional had been all business. He'd never think of addressing Anthony by his nickname. Anthony asked himself again why he'd taken his brother's advice and signed with the newest representative of his former agent's firm. Paul had said Nyles would be "hungry." He hadn't thought that meant "hungry" for common sense.

"Oh, yeah. I'm sorry, man. It's just your nickname's so cool. Why don't you like it?" Nyles sounded sincere.

Anthony drained his second glass of cold water. He wasn't in a chatty mood. The clock was ticking and he was dripping sweat all over his kitchen's white oak hardwood flooring. He also was getting cold.

"Why are you calling, Nyles?" The pinging in the background sounded like metal tapping against porcelain. Nyles was eating. His agent struggled to do one thing well at a time. He didn't like dealing with Nyles when he tried multitasking.

Anthony stacked his now empty glass in his stainless steel dishwasher, then leaned against the gray veined, white marble counter top. His outdoor roof terrace was on the other side of the glass doors that led from his kitchen. That terrace gave him a view of the Brooklyn Museum, Brooklyn Botanical Gardens and Prospect Park; three of his favorite hometown landmarks.

"Oh, yeah." Nyles cleared his throat. "I spoke with Paul. He thinks we should renegotiate your contract."

The muscles in the back of Anthony's neck bunched. He rubbed them with his right hand. "You talked with my brother about my contract?"

The younger man stammered. "He called me."

He unclenched his teeth. "If I want my brother to know about my contract, I'll tell him myself."

Anthony toed off his running shoes and stripped off his socks. He collected his footwear, then padded barefoot through his dining room and down the hallway to his silver and black master bedroom.

"I think Paul has a point. The timing's right." Nyles's tone was urgent. "Your role in winning the Monarchs' first-ever championship was critical."

"Hold on." Anthony bounced the cell phone onto his king-sized mattress. He stripped off his gray sweat-soaked wicking jersey before scooping the black cell phone from his bed and entering his bathroom. "Everyone's role was critical to our championship."

"Sure. Sure. But we have a very small window of opportunity to maximize your position." Nyles was almost as breathless as Anthony was at the eighth mile of his ten-mile morning run. "Things could change this season, and then our position wouldn't be as advantageous."

"I don't want to pressure the franchise." Anthony put his cell phone on speaker to continue the call. He dropped his running shorts and leaned naked against his white porcelain bathroom sink. He was growing impatient with this conversation.

"You don't owe the Monarchs anything, not even loyalty. This is about your career."

Anthony turned on the shower. "That's why I need to keep a good relationship with them."

"But Paul said–"

"I don't care what my brother said. I'm staying with the Monarchs. We'll talk about negotiating my contract once the season ends." Anthony rang off with Nyles. He placed his cell phone on the sink counter and stepped into his shower.

He'd set ambitious goals for himself this season: winning another NBA championship, convincing his brother to let him manage his own career and persuading Faith to accept his apology.

Could he go three for three?

***

"I've got an update on your contract, kiddo." Faith's agent's voice was brisk and emotionless when she called shortly before nine o'clock on Wednesday morning. Faith had a sense of foreboding. For her agent, Lareeta Hearns, "update" was code for "bad news."

"Let me get to the breakroom." Faith rose from her desk at Burnston & Banner, LLC, the accounting firm where she'd worked for almost six years. She wasn't comfortable taking personal calls on the job, especially when they involved her alter ego.

Faith scanned her surroundings as she passed through the reception area and moved toward the rear breakroom. Burnston & Banner's office stank of old world wealth and privilege. It was a sea of scarlet wall-to-wall carpeting and gleaming mahogany wood in which the humming of printers and the cooing of telephones faded into the background.

Faith walked into the empty breakroom, past the conversation area with its dark wood coffee table, and large scarlet cloth sofa and matching armchairs. The blonde wood circular lunch tables arranged across the white linoleum flooring were surrounded by red and gold plastic chairs.

Faith held her cell phone against her ear with her left hand and leaned against the linoleum counter. "They said no, didn't they?"

Lareeta's typing stopped. "Sorry, kiddo. The Horn refused to increase your contract. Claimed you don't have a big enough fan base." Her tone held skepticism, accentuated by the impatient fingernail drumming Faith detected in the background.

For the past four years, Faith had contracted with the New York Horn, a local community daily newspaper, to write and illustrate her BKLYN Crew. The comic strip, written as F. Holmes – her mother's maiden name - chronicled the adventures of three politically savvy and socially conscious third graders, and their friends and family who were all born and raised in Brooklyn.

She'd expected that response but the reality was harsher than she'd anticipated. Each rejection seemed to increase the distance between her current circumstances and her goal of being able to support herself with her comic strips. "Did they give any idea of how many followers they think I should have?"

"No and I didn't ask." Lareeta's tough talk accompanied faster and louder fingernail drumming. "We're done with the Horn. If they don't appreciate you, we'll move on to someone who does."

Faith's eyes stretched. The conversation had taken an unexpected turn. "You want to submit the BKLYN Crew to other papers?"

"No." Lareeta was definite. "We're going to pull the BKLYN Crew from the Horn, and offer it to publishing companies and television producers."

"Pull it from the Horn?" Faith's voice squeaked. "But if we do that, I could lose the few readers I have. We don't even know how long it'll be out of circulation."

She paced the length of the cream counter from end to end, from coffee maker to microwave and back. The firm had better appliances than she had at home. It also had better furniture.

"You won't lose fans." Lareeta sounded confident. "In fact, once the new publisher releases a compilation of your comic strips, your readership will explode."

"*If* we get a publisher to buy my series." Faith's grip tightened on her scarlet cell phone. The taste of dread was sour on her tongue. "This is a very risky proposition."

"It's not. Your series is smart and thought-provoking. Your characters are fun and relatable. Our challenge is to find the right venue for it. Obviously, the Horn is the wrong one. I'm sorry we wasted so much time on them."

Lareeta's support was a balm to Faith's heart, which had been battered by the Horn's rejection. But her proposal was scary in its perilousness.

"I need to think this over." Faith glanced at her Tinker Bell wristwatch. It was almost nine o'clock, the hour the firm opened for business. She needed to get back to her desk.

"Your goal is to support yourself as a cartoonist. I want that for you." Lareeta's sincerity was almost hypnotic, but Faith had her reservations.

"Pulling the strip is like taking a leap of faith without a backup plan."

"That's why it's called a leap of faith."

Faith had confidence in her strip. What she didn't have was Lareeta's risk tolerance, perhaps because she had more at stake.

"Just give me a day or two to consider this."

She and Lareeta ended the call. Back at her desk, Faith struggled to collect her thoughts. They'd flown everywhere on the winds of the Horn's rejection of her request for more money, Lareeta's recommendation that they pull her comic strip from the paper, and her proposal to shop her series to book publishers and television producers.

What should I do? What's my next move?

"Could we speak somewhere in private?" A smooth baritone sounded beside her, sending a shiver up her spine. Only then did Faith notice how quiet the office suite had become.

She looked around to see Anthony Chambers standing next to her desk. The tall, slender NBA athlete made his silver and black Monarchs warm-up suit look like evening wear. Her gaze lifted to his movie star features. Her thoughts once again scattered to the winds.

CHAPTER 4

"Is there somewhere we could speak in private?" Anthony repeated his request to Faith. She looked as though she didn't believe he was there.

It was just after nine o'clock on Wednesday morning. He wanted to get to the Monarchs' practice facility by noon. But first, he needed a large chunk of that time to persuade Faith to forgive him.

Anthony was growing aware of other stares in his direction. The two nearby administrative assistants – one man and one woman – had frozen when they saw him walk into the suite. Other employees had stepped out of their offices. They loitered in the reception area even as they pretended not to see him.

Faith finally noticed the attention they'd drawn. She threw a scowl around the office that sent her gawking coworkers back to work.

Only then did she direct her frown to Anthony. "Come with me."

She led him to the back of the office to a large, bright area with comfortable furnishings and modern appliances. Faith confronted him from the far end of the room. "What are you doing here?"

Anthony's gaze traveled from her tight bun barely visible at the nape of Faith's neck to the pale pink blouse and light gray, pencil slim skirt that outlined her willowy figure. "You look so different from the woman I met on the practice court and the one who was at Connie's birthday party. How's that possible?"

Faith blinked. "I don't think you're here for small talk."

Anthony pulled himself together. "I've come to apologize."

Faith gave him a dubious look. "You've already said you were sorry."

"You didn't accept my initial apology. I distinctly remember that. I've come to offer a better one." Anthony paced forward, shrinking the distance between them to about two arm's lengths. His sneakered steps were silent on the white linoleum flooring.

"I didn't come down with the last rain, Saint." Faith crossed her arms. "You said you were sorry, but you didn't apologize. Which one are you supposed to do to fulfill your obligation to Serge and Troy?"

Anthony really disliked that nickname. He took one step closer and caught her soft scent. "I'm not here out of an obligation."

"You're not?" She'd packed those two little words with a lot of skepticism.

"You were right not to accept my first apology. I didn't understand the effect my words and actions had on you that afternoon, not until you explained it to me. Now that I do understand, I realize that I owe you a much more sincere apology. Will you give me another chance?"

Anthony remained still as Faith searched his features. The tension built in his neck and shoulders, but he waited for her verdict with a steady stare.

"I accept your apology. Thank you." Her words were quiet and gracious.

"Really?" He sought his answer in her eyes.

"Yes, really." Her warm smile nearly rendered him speechless. Nearly.

"I don't know." Anthony rubbed his freshly shaved jawline. "I don't feel forgiven."

Her startled laughter strummed the muscles in his abdomen. "I don't control your feelings." She checked her wristwatch. "Now, I need to get back to work."

Anthony glanced at her timepiece. *Was that an image of Tinker Bell on her watch? What's the story there?*

"Have dinner with me." He hadn't planned the request but he didn't regret it. Now that she'd forgiven him, perhaps they could start over.

Faith looked puzzled. "There's no need for us to have dinner."

"I won't feel like you've forgiven me unless you let me take you to dinner." The more Anthony considered this idea, the more he liked it. "Luke seventeen-three, 'If thy brother trespass against thee, rebuke him, and if he repent, forgive him.'"

"Romans chapter three, verse twenty-three, 'For all have sinned and come short of the glory of God.' I get that and I've forgiven you. Dinner's not necessary." Faith stepped around him, heading back toward the door.

Anthony moved to block her exit. "Break bread with me to absolve me of my transgressions."

"Wow, Serge and Troy must be riding you hard to get you to apologize." Faith eyed him suspiciously.

"This doesn't have anything to do with them." He tried a winning smile. "Please?"

Faith's gaze swept the empty room before returning to Anthony. "I'm not interested in a relationship, if that's where this is going."

Anthony spread his arms and shrugged, ignoring the pinch of disappointment. "I'm just asking for a meal. How about tomorrow night, around eight? I'll pick you up."

"All right, but nothing fancy. Let's go someplace you'd go with your teammates. And we have to make it an early night. I'll have work the next morning." She passed Anthony to lead him from the breakroom.

"Thank you, Faith." His footsteps felt lighter as he followed her to an exit that bypassed the main reception area.

She must not want her coworkers checking him out again. Anthony considered Faith's graceful figure in her conservative skirt and blouse as she walked ahead of him. He was used to being paraded around like a status object, even by his brother. Faith's actions made him feel like a regular person. It was a good feeling, one he could get used to.

***

Anthony poured himself a second glass of cold water from the filtered silver faucet at his kitchen sink Thursday morning. His breathing had returned to normal and his body temperature was starting to cool from his ten-mile run. Staying in shape during the off season meant not having to work as hard to get back into competitive condition once the regular season started. He'd need that extra edge if the Brooklyn Monarchs were to defend their championship.

Back-to-back titles.

Anything's possible.

He'd finished half of his second serving of water from the sixteen-ounce glass when his cell phone buzzed. Anthony drew the device from the Velcro pocket of his black running shorts.

The caller identification screen displayed his agent's personal cell phone number. This was becoming a habit.

"What's going on, Nyles?" Anthony drank more water. His body craved it.

"Tony, my man, how's it goin'?" Nyles must have decided they were friends. Anthony let it go.

"I'm fine. What's up?" Anthony drained his water, then set the glass in his dishwasher. He leaned back against his gray marble counter and stared through his kitchen's glass doors in the direction of Prospect Park.

"I think we should revisit the whole renegotiating your contract thing." In the background, Nyles's microwave oven sounded. Did his agent ever cook real meals?

"Have you been talking with Paul again?" Anthony's sports watch read almost a quarter after eight A.M. He toed off his running shoes, then pulled off his sweat soaked socks.

"No, Sai..., Tony. I just think it would be worth looking at it more closely."

Anthony disagreed. "We'll deal with my contract when it comes up for renegotiation at the end of the season. Is there anything else?" He scooped up his shoes and socks, and headed barefoot to his bedroom.

A clinking noise sounded in the background. Nyles was having breakfast.

"You were rushed when we spoke on Wednesday. But I really think you should give this renegotiation thing some serious thought. This is a critical situation."

"Critical for whom?" It didn't escape Anthony's notice that his agent's percentage would increase with his richer contract.

He pressed the speaker icon on his cell phone screen, then set the device on his sink counter. His hands were now free to strip off his sweat-soaked navy wicking jersey and black running shorts.

"It's critical for us – for *you*." Nyles sounded urgent. "This isn't about just one contract. This is your career."

"I know." Anthony leaned naked against his bathroom sink. "And I've told you that I want to spend it with the Monarchs."

"But does Jackie Jones want you on the Monarchs roster for the long term?" Nyles's question was fair.

Anthony wasn't going to tell his agent that he'd wondered – and worried - about that, too. When they'd drafted him after college, he'd loved the franchise. At first, it had felt like a family, close knit, caring. They weren't just players, they were people.

Sure, they'd experienced some rocky years when the surviving founding owner, Franklin Jones, had become ill. But his granddaughter had taken control of the franchise and was rebuilding it the way her grandfather would have wanted. Anthony wanted to be a part of that again.

His gaze moved over his spacious master bathroom. Remodeling the room in silver and black accents, the Monarchs team colors, was a tribute to the franchise. It was carried out in the floor tile and the trim in the glass enclosed shower-and-soak-tub combination.

"My goal is to work hard enough to make myself indispensable to the team." Anthony could hear Nyles' silverware scrapping against his porcelain dishes. He was getting hungry himself.

"But how do you know the Monarchs will be as loyal to you." Nyles sounded like he was talking with his mouth full. "And what if you get injured? At least let me test the waters about a possible contract renegotiation."

Anthony hesitated. Maybe Nyles and Paul had a point.

Suppose he was injured this season – or next season? He wasn't the only employee dependent upon the franchise's success. If he sustained an injury, Anthony couldn't blame the Monarchs if it picked up a healthier player and didn't renew his contract. It made good business sense for the franchise.

But not for me.

He sighed, rubbing the knotted muscles at the back of his neck. He was torn between what he wanted to do – remain with the team – and what he should do – protect his career.

He picked up his cell phone and tapped the speaker icon to disengage the feature. He held the device to his ear. "I'm still not convinced that renegotiating early is a good idea, but it wouldn't hurt to get a sense of Jackie's thoughts about my future with the team."

"Great!" Nyles was a little too enthusiastic. "I'll get right on it."

"Nyles, just make sure you don't mess things up for me with the Monarchs. I mean it."

"I won't. If anything, the Monarchs won't know what hit them."

Anthony was the opposite of reassured. "That's not what I mean. Don't hit the Monarchs. Just test the waters."

"It was just a figure of speech, Sai...Tony." Nyles paused as though pulling himself together. "I'll just get Jackie's thoughts about your contract. That's it."

"Good." Anthony ended the call with a nagging sense of unease.

CHAPTER 5

"You've been bouncing off the walls since you arrived." Serge followed Constance from his kitchen Thursday evening. "Are you finally going to tell me why?"

She'd made him wait until they'd finished dinner and tidied up before she'd share her news. Curiosity was suffocating him.

The aromas from their spicy chicken and steamed vegetable dinner followed him as Constance led him to the loveseat in his living room. With training camp less than three weeks away, he wanted to eat healthier meals, but that didn't mean they had to be boring.

Constance smoothed her modest pink floral tea dress almost nervously. The skirt fluttered around her knees as she settled close beside him on the plump gray linen canvas cushion. She took his big, calloused hands in her small, soft ones. He wondered at the lights dancing in her grass green eyes.

Constance shifted toward him. Her high cheekbones were flushed. Her eyes were sparkling. "My divorce is final."

Serge grabbed Constance to him. Happiness exploded through him like fireworks on Bastille Day. He was as excited as a school boy on Christmas morning; as anxious as a top pick on the NBA's draft day; as exhilarated as when his team had won the championship.

Now nothing stood in the way of their getting married!

He held Constance to his heart. "This is wonderful news."

"I know!" Constance leaned back to grin up at him. "I thought Wade would fight it a lot harder than he did. I overestimated my value."

How could she think that?

"*Non*. It's impossible to overestimate your worth. You're priceless, but he never realized that." Serge shrugged a shoulder. "His loss."

"You're sweet." She cupped the side of his face with her warm hand. It trembled just a bit.

The homeless shelter where Constance and Tiffany had lived when they'd first arrived from Iowa had helped Constance file the divorce papers immediately. Her ex-husband's response had been to try to intimidate her by showing up at the apartment Constance and Tiffany shared with Andrea and Faith.

Constance had not been intimidated.

Serge was drowning in feelings: joy, gratitude, love. He had to get himself under control before he either fainted or blurted his marriage proposal right here, right now, ruining everything. He tugged his gaze from hers and drew several deep breaths.

On his right, a wide picture window shielded by sheer white curtains offered a view overlooking Prospect Park, the Brooklyn Botanical Gardens and the Brooklyn Museum.

His eyes swept his living room: the classic gray canvas linen sofa, a match to the loveseat, and the twin high-back chairs; the walnut wood flooring; and paper white walls. The stark surroundings set a brilliant contrast to the impressionistic paintings that exploded color on his walls.

The dining room behind them was dominated by a walnut wood table with six matching ebony velvet-padded chairs. Enough to accommodate a large family. The image of Constance and himself at the table surrounded by Tiffany, and her brothers and sisters filled Serge with pleasure.

Both the living and dining rooms were comfortable spaces, if long and somewhat narrow. Less than a week before, he'd welcomed the more than sixty people who'd helped celebrate Constance's twenty-sixth birthday here. Although perhaps they should rent a hall for the wedding reception. He could envision them inviting twice as many guests to that event.

Edith Piaf's dreamy French love song, *"Hymne à L'Amour,"* played softly through his wireless Bluetooth speaker. The title translated to "The Hymn to Love." It would be perfect for their first dance. Would Constance agree?

Serge turned back to find Constance also gazing around the living room. Were her thoughts the same as his? "I'm so happy for you." *And for me.* "Now you can start planning for your future."

His words were a tentative first step toward what he hoped would be a welcomed marriage proposal. He'd bought the ring just a little more than a month after meeting Constance. It was love at first sight, at least for him. He'd been that confident that he wanted to share his life with her and Tiffany.

"Planning my future." Constance drew an unsteady breath. She slipped her hands from his and rose from the sofa. "It sounds so wonderful yet it feels so overwhelming."

"In what way?" Serge shifted to watch her wander the room. *Should I get the ring now?*

Constance crossed to the stone-and-walnut-wood fireplace and stared into its darkness. "I never thought I'd be free of him.

I thought I'd be his wife until the day that I died and that he would kill me."

Her words were a cold, steel blade in his chest. His mind wiped clean. Constance had such quiet strength. It was a shock to learn that she'd lived so long with such debilitating fear.

Serge had met her ex-husband. Wade was at least six inches taller than her and almost a hundred pounds heavier. He'd used that size to hurt this gentle, caring woman. Serge wanted to sprint to Iowa and knock the crap out of him. Then wake him up and pummel him again.

"You hadn't realized that you could leave him?"

Constance faced Serge. "And go where?"

In the five months that they'd been together, since April, they'd never discussed this part of her past. He'd wanted to because he cared for her and Tiffany. That was also the reason he hadn't pushed. Now she was opening that door to him. With caution and respect, he stepped through. "Why didn't you go to your mother?"

Besides Tiffany, Bettie Lee Maddox was the only living relative Constance had. Serge didn't know much about her.

"I did go to her. Several times. She always sent me back." Constance returned her attention to the fireplace. She ran her fingers over some of the framed photos on the mantel. "Mother believes a man has the right to hit his wife."

"*Merde*." Serge no longer wanted to know Bettie Lee Maddox.

Constance tossed a smile over her shoulder. "I don't know much French, but I have a feeling that's not a nice word."

He'd say it again if she gave him another smile like that one. "Wasn't there anyone to help you? No friends that you could go to?"

Constance picked up the photo of him, sitting on the grass with her and Tiffany at the Botanical Gardens earlier in the summer. Was she remembering the wonderful time they'd had that day? He always had a great time with them, whether they were touring Brooklyn or doing laundry.

"I had to find the courage to help myself." Constance returned the photo to the mantel.

That courage had come when Wade had threatened their daughter. The difference between Constance and her mother was stark. When Constance went to her mother for protection from her abusive husband, Bettie Lee had sent her back into the danger. But when that abuser became violent toward her own daughter, Constance had found the courage to protect her child even though she had no resources and no plan.

Serge stood to join Constance in front of the fireplace. He ran his hand over her shoulder-length hair, the color of the sun. "I'm very proud of you."

She gave him an unsteady smile. "Thank you.

"Now that you've tossed Wade out of your life, what do you want to do next?" The realization hurt, but Serge recognized that his dream of building a life with Constance and Tiffany would have to wait. This time wasn't about him. It was about Constance and whatever she needed to feel whole again.

The dark clouds had lifted from Constance's grass green eyes. A look of wonder had returned. "I don't know. I feel as though I have all of these possibilities. I've never had so many options before."

Serge smiled. Her enthusiasm was contagious. "Tell me about one."

"Well..." Constance took his hand and led him to one of his high-backed armchairs. He sat, and she settled onto his lap. "I enjoy helping Troy with the marketing campaigns and want to be more involved in them."

"What's stopping you?" Serge leaned his head against the back of the chair and studied her animated features.

"I don't have a degree. The franchise offers college tuition assistance to full-time employees, though." Constance took a deep breath. "Maybe I'll look into applying to college."

"*Non.*" Serge shook his head. "No 'maybes.' If this is something that you want to do, you must do it."

Constance's green eyes were cautious. "Suppose I fail?"

"You won't. You have the will to succeed. You've already proven that."

"All right." She offered a self-deprecating laugh. "It may take me ten years to get the degree, but it would be so worth it."

Serge froze in horror. Ten years? *Non. Non. Non.* He couldn't wait ten years to marry Constance. He just couldn't.

He took her hand and kissed her palm. "Connie, together, we'll get you that degree in much, *much* less time."

Serge held her eyes. *That,* ma chere, *is a promise.*

Chapter 6

Anthony's definition of "casual dining" and hers were so far apart from each other, Faith wondered whether they spoke different languages. It's a good thing she wore her all-purpose little black dress.

With his large warm hand at the small of her back, Anthony escorted Faith to the restaurant's hostess station Thursday evening. "Chambers. I have a reservation for two."

The tall young woman with a wealth of dishwater blond hair piled precariously on top of her head looked up. She wore what appeared to be a uniform: bright white blouse, opened at the neck and a black matador jacket.

She gave Anthony a discreet smile of recognition. When her attention turned to Faith, the expression in her light brown eyes changed. *I know you bought that dress at a thrift shop.*

Faith was amused. She gave the young hostess a once over. *I'd advise against throwing stones while wearing that outfit. You look like you're about to perform circus tricks.*

The hostess stiffened, then turned to collect the menus. "This way, please." She avoided eye contact with Faith for the rest of their encounter.

Faith's three-inch stilettos tapped across the hardwood floor as she followed the hostess. She sensed Anthony close behind her. Perhaps too close.

The restaurant's lighting was dim, adding a touch of romance to the surroundings. The tables actually had cloths. The crisp white fabric looked starched. Each centerpiece was beautiful, a tall cylinder candle surrounded by fresh marigolds in a ceramic vase.

Faith was relieved to see that the fancy restaurant served human portions instead of sampler sizes. Tantalizing scents floated from the tables: rich sauces, savory soups, well-seasoned meats, sautéed seafoods and fresh vegetables. The aromas weakened her resolved to eat healthily. Her mind lectured, *"Small portions."* Her stomach demanded, *"Bring it on! Bring it!"*

The hostess led them past the booths and tables for two in the main dining area to a more exclusive section. Here, there were private booths for two off the aisle. Faith took the slight step up. Anthony held her chair. Once he'd taken his seat, the hostess gave them their menus. She seemed relieved to excuse herself.

Faith flicked a look toward Anthony before opening her menu. "I can't see you taking Serge to a place like this."

Anthony's lips twitched and his eyes twinkled at her before returning to the menu. "Neither can I."

As much as she didn't want to admit it, Faith was having a hard time keeping her eyes off her companion. He looked amazing in his slim fit wool blend suit. The dark green color complimented his olive eyes and warmed his golden skin. She wanted to reach out and stroke his firm, square chin.

"You look wonderful." *Warning: Outer voice.* Embarrassed, Faith tucked her attention back into her menu.

"Thank you. So do you." His sincerity eased her discomfort.

They were interrupted by their server, a young man in a uniform similar to the hostess'. He brought their breads and took their drink orders. They both requested ice water.

"You don't drink?" Curiosity lit Anthony's eyes.

"Not tonight." She softened her response with a smile.

Anthony responded with a cheeky expression. "Ah, you need to keep your wits about you. I'm flattered."

"Don't be." Faith's tone was parched. "Why aren't you drinking?"

"We're less than three weeks from training camp and we have a title to defend."

Faith remembered how exuberant Brooklyn had been with the Monarchs' first title in its storied franchise history. Even quasi-fans had lost their collective minds. "Do you think you can repeat as league champions?"

"Yes." His response was unequivocal.

Faith tilted her head. "What makes you so confident?"

"Because we've proven to ourselves that we're capable." Anthony lowered his menu and leaned into the table. "We've endured years of coming close only to return empty handed. There were so many years when we didn't even make the playoffs. But last season, we broke our culture of losing and proved to ourselves and the league that we could win."

Faith could feel his determination. "I hope you do repeat. It would be great for the franchise and for Brooklyn."

She returned to the comparative safety of the menu. Faith didn't want to fall victim to the baller's undeniable good looks and his burgeoning charm. He was intelligent, passionate. And the man knew his bible.

In self-defense, she focused on the restaurant's menu. The entrees featured meats, chicken and fish, with side dishes of potatoes, rice pilaf, vegetables, salads and soups. With those main courses, the appetizers seemed like overkill and dessert would be out of the question - unless Anthony was willing to roll her out of there.

The costs had a dampening effect on her appetite, though. She could make a lot of these dishes for less than a third of what the establishment was charging. But tonight, after dinner, she wouldn't have to clean up. Priceless.

It didn't take long for their server to return with their glasses of ice water. He then invited them to give him their selections. Faith requested the crab stuffed flounder with peas, carrots and corn. Anthony chose the hickory smoked chicken also with vegetables.

Anthony turned his attention to Faith as their young server hurried away. "Thank you for having dinner with me."

"Thank *you*. This place is...incredible." Also a fitting description for him. "You didn't need to do all of this." Faith waved a hand to encompass their surroundings.

"Yes, I did."

Casual conversation entertained them until their server returned with their entrées, then carried them through most of the meal. Faith was actually disappointed when the young man cleared their dishes and returned with their bill. Anthony's company, the meal, everything had been better than she'd expected and much more than she'd hoped for. If she kept a diary, tonight would warrant a two-page entry.

"There's something I've been wondering." Anthony tucked his credit card back into his wallet. He signed the final bill, then returned it to the padded black leather check presenter. "Who are you really? Every time I see you, you appear to be a different person."

"What do you mean?" Faith took a long drink from the glass of water their server had refilled.

A teasing smile curved Anthony's well-shaped lips. "I thought you were a flirt when we first met on the practice court."

Faith swallowed quickly before she choked. She set her glass down. "I was *not* flirting with you."

"It kinda felt like you were."

"I don't control your feelings."

Anthony continued. "You looked like a temptress at Connie's birthday party."

"Tempting whom?"

"Me, of course."

"*Why* would I do that?"

"Oh, ouch! Heart, meet dagger."

"What are you talking about?" Faith's mind spun at this turn in his conversation.

Anthony continued as though she hadn't spoken. "Yesterday at your office, you were all business from your pulled-back hair to your sensible shoes." His eyes lifted to her hair, which she'd worn loose tonight.

"That reminds me, don't come to the firm again."

"And tonight, you're a siren."

"What does that even mean?"

He grinned. "It means that I need to be more careful around you."

"Well, that's a given."

Anthony spread his hands. "Now that we've identified the many personas of Faith Wilcox–"

"There's only one me."

Anthony leaned into the table, claiming her gaze. "Who are you really?"

He seemed sincerely interested. That blew Faith's mind. Even scarier: She wanted to tell him. It was the look in his eyes. It hypnotized her, drawing confidences she wouldn't ordinarily share. "I'm a cartoonist."

"Editorial cartoons or graphic novels?"

Faith grinned. "Comic strips, like Aaron MacGruder's 'Boondocks.'" She set down her glass of water and used her hands to help her explain. "I use my characters to express what I see as the humor or humorous contradictions in society's ordinary assumptions."

Anthony looked puzzled. "Could you give me an example?"

"My characters are elementary school kids of different ethnicities. In one exchange, for example, one of the African American kids complains that she's tired of African Americans leaving the hood for the 'burbs every time they get some money. She says, 'Someone's gotta stay back.' Another kid responds, 'What are you talking about? *You're* from the 'burbs.' That exchange challenges the belief that African Americans only live in urban areas, and only white people live in the suburbs or rural communities when in fact some African Americans were born and raised in suburbs and rural communities."

Anthony's jaw dropped. His eyes grew wide. He lowered his arms to the table and gaped at Faith as though she was an alien who'd just teleported to his table. "That was last week's BKLYN Crew strip. You're F. Holmes."

Faith was even more shocked than Anthony looked. "Someone actually reads it."

"Of course! Paul and I enjoy it. A lot of the players read it, too."

"I'm flattered." *Understatement.* So often, Faith felt as though her strip just filled an empty space in the New York Horn. To meet someone who actually followed her series – and enjoyed it! – was overwhelming.

Anthony gave her a dazed grin. “I can’t believe that I’m having dinner with a celebrity.”

Faith laughed. “That sounds so odd coming from an NBA champion.”

“Do you write *and* illustrate the story?”

“Yes, I do.”

“So why are you working at an accounting firm?”

Reality had such an ugly way of bursting someone’s bubble. “Producing comic strips while gratifying, doesn’t pay the bills, at least not yet.”

“It will soon.” Anthony leaned back on his seat. “You’ve got a lot of talent. What’re doing to grow your audience?”

“My agent wants to shop the Crew to publishers and production companies, but I’m not sure I’m ready.”

“Of course you are.” Anthony looked surprised. “The BKLYN Crew needs a national audience. You’re not getting that with the Horn. Even in New York, it has a limited distribution.”

“But to pull the strip from the Horn to wait to see if someone else wants it is a risk that I don’t know that I’m ready for.” Faith worried her bottom lip.

“If this is what you want, you have to take some risks. Nothing worth having comes easily.”

Faith sat back on her chair and considered Anthony more closely. “What are we doing here, Tony?”

“I told you.” He gave her a puzzled look. “I asked you to dinner to apologize properly.”

“That’s it? Because it feels like something more.”

"Would that be so bad? I think you're interesting, and I'd like to get to know you better." A warm glow entered his olive eyes, making Faith's heart skip one or two – or three – beats.

She'd been thinking the same thing about him, but the timing was wrong. She had a lot to accomplish before she could focus on a personal life.

"I'm sorry, Tony. As I said yesterday, a relationship's not in the cards for me right now." But she was starting to wish she'd been dealt a different hand.

Anthony considered her for a long silent moment. "If not a relationship, then how about a friendship?"

What was that advice country music singer Kenny Rogers had offered gamblers? Know when to hold, fold, walk away and run.

Faith ignored it. "I'd like that." Hopefully, at the end of this hand, she wouldn't end up writing a bunch of IOUs to her future.

CHAPTER 7

Early Friday morning, Faith's black pumps tapped across the white tiled flooring in the lobby of the building that housed the Burnston & Banner accounting firm. On the other end of the cell phone connection, her agent chastised and encouraged her in the same breath.

"So have you made up your mind yet, because seriously, watching grass grow is more productive." Lareeta's yawn didn't even sound real.

"It's only been two days." Faith had arrived early to have this conversation with her agent before she had to be at her desk at nine A.M. She checked her Tinker Bell wristwatch. She still had a few minutes.

"No, Faith. It's been three years." Lareeta's tone was somber. "That's how long the Horn has been publishing the BKLYN Crew. It's past time we made a move."

Beneath her agent's autocratic tone, Faith heard the swirling notes of a classical arrangement. Years ago, Lareeta had told her that she found Chopin's compositions soothing. It wasn't yet nine o'clock. What had happened to agitate her agent this early in the morning?

"But is this the right move?" Faith lifted her hand in greeting to a few coworkers who were standing at the front of the lobby near the elevators.

Of course, Lareeta was right. It was time to fish or cut bait with the Horn, but a lot was at stake. It was her lifelong dream to support herself as a cartoonist. She wanted to achieve it not just for herself but for her parents. This was her priority before she could consider anything else, such as a serious relationship with a handsome, exciting professional athlete.

"Faith, in my business, we put a price tag on the things we value." Lareeta was tapping her pen against her desk. "Based on the final offer letter the Horn sent this morning, they don't value you."

Now she knew what had annoyed her agent. It was a body blow to Faith's confidence. She leaned back against the cold tiled wall in the rear of the building's lobby. "If the Horn's not committed to the Crew after all this time, what makes you think a publisher or producer would be interested?"

"The Horn's cheap." Lareeta's tone was blunt with residual anger. "They know you're worth more, but they're deliberately lowballing us. It wouldn't take much to find you a better home."

"What'll happen to my readers if my strip disappears from the newspaper and its website?" Faith tried to keep the panic from her voice. She wasn't confident she was succeeding. "Won't they forget about me?"

"They're following you on social media." She could almost see Lareeta rolling her eyes. "Tell them what's going on. And would it kill you to start a reader enewsletter as I've suggested?"

"You mean nagged."

"Whatever it takes." Lareeta sighed. "Look, I don't have a crystal ball. Life doesn't come with guarantees. Insert any cliché that works for you here. The bottom line is the Horn doesn't respect you. Why would you continue to cast your pearls before these swine?"

What should I do? What was the best next move for me?

Faith wanted to pull her hair out by the roots. "Lareeta, I know you're right, but my risk-averse nature is afraid of taking this leap before I've looked."

"But you *have* looked." Lareeta sounded as though she was throwing up her hands, although Faith knew she couldn't do that without dropping her phone. "You've looked for so long and so hard that you've developed tunnel vision."

Once again, Lareeta was right. She hadn't realized all the things she was missing out on while she put her life on hold under the guise of chasing her dream. This wasn't supposed to be a hobby. It was meant to be her livelihood. As much as she loved Andrea, Constance and Tiffany – and she did love them – she had to be able to pay her bills without depending on roommates to help her get by.

I'd like to get to know you better. Anthony's voice slipped unbidden into her mind. She'd like to get to know him, too. He was interesting, fun and sexy as all get out. She didn't want to put the chance of a relationship with him on the back burner.

If this is what you want, you have to take some risks. Nothing worth having comes easily.

Faith heard Anthony's voice as though he was standing beside her. She drew a deep breath. "All right. If the Horn doesn't value the BKLYN Crew, then we'll find an outlet that will. Surely, there's someone out there besides you, me and my Mom who could share my vision for the Crew."

Lareeta grunted. "Finally. I'll be in touch." The line went dead before Faith could say goodbye, but she wasn't offended. That was just Lareeta's way.

Faith imagined that, right now, Lareeta was calling the Horn. The newspaper understood that, if Faith rejected their offer, she was free to pursue other interests. That's what she was doing – and it felt great.

She slipped her cell phone into her oversized bronze purse and made it to the bank of elevators toward the front of the lobby with minutes to spare. The future was yet unwritten. The uncertainty was scary, but when Faith pushed past the fear, she saw endless possibilities.

An image of Anthony Chambers flirted across her mind. *Endless possibilities.*

***

Anthony raced up the first four flights of the twenty-story building in downtown Brooklyn late Friday morning to the offices where his agent worked. He hadn't broken a sweat and he was barely out of breath. His sneakered feet had been silent on the metal steps. The morning's sports section of the New York Horn was crumpled in his right fist. He'd hoped to work off at least some of the righteous rage coursing through his bloodstream. The effort had failed. Decisively.

He pushed his way through the heavy metal stairwell door and into the gold and white marbled antechamber beside the bank of gold elevators. To his right were the glass doors that opened onto Players' Personnel Agency, LLC, the firm that represented him and employed Nyles Todd, his soon-to-be ex-agent.

Anthony paused to adjust his black polyester warm-up jacket and the crisp silver cotton T-shirt underneath. He was wearing the warmup suit because he still intended to start his workout by eleven A.M. That gave him an hour to fire Nyles and get to the Monarchs' practice facility.

He yanked open the office door. The gold-plated handle was cold against his palm.

Anthony nodded to the redheaded receptionist seated at the front desk as he strode past her. "Nyles's expecting me." *Or at least, he should be.*

"Um, Mister Chambers, um, I could announce you." The young woman's anxious voice trailed after him as he marched down the gold carpeted hallway. The suite stank of wealth accumulated from the blood, sweat, tears and injuries of others.

"No need."

She was probably on the phone with Nyles now anyway. That wasn't the point. After the stunt Nyles had pulled, Anthony wasn't going to wait for an audience with his agent before he ripped him a new one.

Anthony shoved through his agent's half-opened door. He strode across the plush gold carpeting to Nyles's honey wood modular desk.

He pressed the telephone's switch hook to disconnect the call, then slapped the front page of the Horn's sports section face up on the desk. "What have you done?"

The page included an action photo of Anthony taken during game seven of last season's NBA finals. The headline above the picture read, FANS RAGE AT CHAMBERS' DEMAND FOR MORE CASH.

Blood drained from Nyles's face as he lifted his gaze to Anthony's. "I'm sorry, Sai–Tony. I must have let it leak to the media that you were thinking about renegotiating your contract."

"You *must* have?" Anthony held up the paper. "I'm thinking it's a pretty safe bet that you did."

"I'm sorry, Tony, but the public will support you."

"Did you read the story? It's right in the headline. Not only are fans *unsupportive*. They're *raging* against me." Anthony backed away from the desk before he did something regrettable.

"I can turn this around. Don't worry." Nyles's words ran together. Anthony could almost smell the younger man's fear.

Nyles was about a foot shorter than Anthony and stocky. His lank dirty blonde hair was conservatively cut. His small blue-gray eyes were watchful in his pale round face. He was a nice young guy who meant well. The problem was Nyles wasn't an independent thinker and negotiations weren't his strength.

Why did I allow Paul to convince me to sign a contract with this kid?

Anthony closed the office door before facing Nyles again, this time from across the room. "How did this happen?"

Nyles's reluctance to make his confession was palpable. He loosened his brown tie, which matched almost exactly the brown suit jacket hanging from his black coatrack.

"I called Jackie on Thursday after you and I had talked. Remember I told you that I was going to do that?" Nyles continued when Anthony remained silent. "I told her that you and I wanted to renegotiate your contract."

"And?"

"She wasn't very receptive to the idea. Well, she wasn't receptive at all. She pointed out that you still have this season on your contract, and that the Monarchs' policy was not to renegotiate active contracts."

Anthony scrubbed his hands over his face. "You should've been prepared for that."

His previous agent would have been.

No, scratch that.

His previous agent would never have suggested renegotiating his contract because he would have known only bad things – like negative articles on the front page sports sections – could come of such a proposal. Anthony wanted to pull his hair out by the roots.

"I was prepared." Nyles had the gumption to sound offended. "That's the reason I contacted the media. I thought it would help to generate public support. I wanted to get your fans on our side."

Incredible.

Anthony looked at the sports section in his hand. "How'd that work out for me?"

"Not well." Nyles sighed.

"That's an understatement." Anthony struggled to keep his tone low and steady. "You were supposed to get an idea of where Jackie was on my contract. Instead you gave Monarchs fans a reason to call me greedy and selfish, two things I've never wanted to be."

"I thought it would make a great story: Hometown Hero Brings Trophy Back to Brooklyn; Now He Wants to Get Paid."

"Most of the Monarchs are hometown heroes." The fact that most of the players were from Brooklyn was one of the few bonds the dysfunctional team had. "Tell Jackie that we're dropping the renegotiation. We'll discuss my new contract during the off-season."

Nyles looked horrified. "But Sai...Tony, we can't announce that we want to renegotiate one day, then change our minds the next. We need to give this some time. Things'll turn around."

Anthony lifted the sports section. "This can't be turned around. This ball's already in play."

"We'll get the public on our side." Nyles's lips were moving, but he wasn't home.

"I'm not renegotiating my contract in the media. When the time comes, we'll work with Jackie and no one else."

Nyles raised a hand as though to stop Anthony's thoughts. "Um, Tony, we're still sort of renegotiating. I can't take the request off the table now. It'll look like we caved and that'll make it harder for us to renegotiate next time."

Anthony's thoughts screeched to a halt. Nyles was finally making sense. Too bad that hadn't happened before his reckless agent nearly tanked his relationship with the Monarchs. Was it greed or idiocy that had blinded the younger man? Either way, what was he going to do now?

***

Showered and dressed after her early Saturday morning jog, Faith entered the kitchen to fix breakfast. She didn't know her roommates' plans for the day so it was breakfast for one. Cereal would do. She set a bowl on the counter, then pulled milk from the refrigerator and her favorite cereal brand from a cupboard.

"Good morning. How was your run?" Constance entered the kitchen with Tiffany in tow. Her daughter scurried over to hug Faith's leg.

"A little rough. Long week." *It had nothing to do with Anthony or the fact that I haven't heard from him since Thursday.*

Faith put her hand on Tiffany's silky blonde hair. "Good morning, Tiff. Did you sleep well?"

"Yesh." The little girl pressed her cheek against Faith's thigh. She looked like a mini-me to her mother in her nearly identical T-shirt and shorts.

"Good morning, everyone." Andrea's greeting preceded her into the kitchen. She remained near the threshold since the kitchen was too small to accommodate the four of them at one time.

Faith gave the reporter's kiwi green romper an admiring once over. The style complimented her roommate's slender figure and long, toned legs. "Do you have time for breakfast?"

"I'm meeting Troy." Andrea smoothed her shoulder-length, dark brown hair. She wore the straight tresses parted in the middle. "With the Monarchs' training camp less than three weeks away, we want to spend as much time together as possible before things get crazy."

"Serge feels the same way." Constance's grass green eyes were dubious as she considered Faith's bowl of cereal. "I'm making eggs for Tiff and me. Would you like me to make some for you? It wouldn't be any trouble."

"No, thanks. I'm fine with cereal this morning." Faith gave Constance a grateful smile before turning to Andrea. "Scheduling time to spend with Troy would be a lot easier if you lived together."

Andrea's gaze drifted away from her roommates. "We've only been together four months."

"You knew each other for years before you started dating." Behind her, Faith could hear Constance and Tiffany getting ready to cook their eggs.

Andrea shifted her legs. Her strappy caramel sandals showed off her pedicure complete with emerald polish. "I want to wait a few more months before moving in together."

Faith searched Andrea's expression. "Is everything OK with the two of you?"

Andrea's sherry brown eyes gaze was startled. "Yes, of course."

"Then why are you acting so jumpy about moving in with him?" Maybe she should mind her own business. This was Andrea and Troy's relationship. They'd decide when they were ready to take the next step. But something was wrong and Faith was concerned.

"I'm not jumpy." Andrea glanced at her black Timex wristwatch. "I should get going. I don't want to be late."

Faith considered the concern on her friend's heart-shaped face. "Andrea, are you dragging your feet because you're afraid Connie and I won't be able to afford the rent without you?"

Andrea froze. "I don't...I never said..."

"Don't put your life on hold for us." Faith waved a dismissive hand. "Connie, Tiff and I can manage on our own, can't we?"

"We'll be fine, Andrea." Connie kept her eyes on the frying pan. The aroma of eggs and butter wafted around the kitchen, giving Faith second thoughts about her breakfast choice.

"And with you out of the picture, Tiff could have her own room." Faith met Andrea's worried gaze again. "In the worst-case scenario, we'll find another roommate."

That wasn't Faith's first option. It would be hard to find someone with whom she could live in this very small apartment. She'd been lucky with Andrea, Constance and Tiffany.

Andrea checked her watch again. "I really need to go, but we'll talk about this more later."

Puzzled, Faith watched Andrea let herself out of the apartment. She took her cereal bowl and followed Constance into the dining area. "What's to talk about? If she wants to move in with

Troy, she should."

Constance placed one of the plates of scrambled eggs and toast in front of Tiffany's chair and carried the other to her seat. "It's not that simple."

Faith sat across from Constance. "Why not?"

Constance met her gaze. "If you had to pay any more than you already do in rent, you wouldn't have any money left. You wouldn't be able to build any savings for an emergency."

The truth hurt, but what hurt even more was knowing her friends were putting their lives on hold because of her financial circumstances. That she simply couldn't bear. "Are you postponing moving in with Serge because of me as well?"

A small smile tipped Constance's lips. "Well, there's the small matter of Tiff. Any move I make affects her. I want to make sure it's the right one. Besides, Serge hasn't shown any interest in anything more than dating."

Faith glanced at the little girl who was happily eating her eggs with a spoon. "You and Andrea are making this more complicated than it needs to be. You should move on with your lives. Don't let me hold you back. One way or the other, everything'll work out."

She escaped to her bedroom, closing the door and throwing herself onto her mattress. There wasn't enough room for pacing. She was embarrassed, upset and – she'd admit it – scared. She'd made a mess of things by waiting for her dream to fall into her lap. Even her roommates felt backed into a corner. But she'd fix this situation, even if it meant giving up her dream and going home to her mother in Georgia.

CHAPTER 8

Faith sprawled on the lumpy, bumpy brown armchair that balanced on the threadbare burnt umber area rug in her living room. The early afternoon sun's efforts to bathe her in its cheerful warmth were wasted. Faith was nursing a serious sulk after realizing her roommates were putting their lives on hold – for her.

What was it about me that made them think they had to? Do I come across as that *much of a loser?*

She expended her dark mood on a progression of developmental sketches for a comic strip character that had recently moved into her mind. For the past few hours, she'd been trying to capture the little boy's physical likeness, but each iteration had been grumpier than the last. The exercise wasn't doing a darned thing for her self-esteem, either. Faith ripped her most recent attempt from her eleven-by-seventeen inch sketchbook, crushed it in her fist, then tossed it across the room to join the growing pile of rejects.

Someone knocked on her apartment door. A distraction; just what she needed. Faith unwrapped herself from the battered armchair. She tossed her sketch book to the sofa, then hurried across her living room and dining area to the door. In her stocking feet, she lifted onto her toes and looked through the peephole to see who'd pulled her from the brink of losing her mind.

Tony!?! How did he know where I live?

She looked down at her oversized lavender T-shirt, baggy orange shorts and purple socks. And what about her hair? Did she want him to see her like this?

Nooo!

It was one thing for neighbors or girlfriends to see her like this, but not a guy she was pretending not to want to impress.

Anthony's second knock was more tentative.

Faith smoothed her hair, then jerked open the door. "I'm not really dressed for guests."

His olive green gaze looked lost. "I can really use some company."

Just like that, her embarrassment was forgotten. She stepped back, pulling the door with her to invite him in. "Can I get you something to drink? I've got orange juice, fruit punch, milk and water."

"Ice water, if it's not too much trouble." He entered the apartment and waited while she locked the door.

"Make yourself comfortable. I'll join you in a moment." Faith gestured toward the living room as she turned into the kitchen.

She filled two glasses from the pitcher of ice water in the refrigerator. She refilled the pitcher, then returned it to the fridge before joining Anthony in her living room.

He was casually dressed in khaki shorts and a winter green, short-sleeved polo shirt. Faith lifted her gaze from his tight and toned body to the clean lines of his near-perfect profile. He seemed perplexed as he stood in her living room, studying her collection of wadded sketch paper.

"Thank you." Anthony accepted the glass from her. He used it to gesture toward her stack of crushed pages. "Am I interrupting something?"

Faith resisted the urge to clean up her mess. It wasn't hurting anyone. "What's wrong, Tony?"

Anthony took a seat on the sofa, which faced the window to their fire escape across the room. "Have you seen any of the articles the Horn has printed about my contract these past two days?"

"I've seen both of them." Faith returned to her armchair. She curled her right leg under her and shifted to face him. "Now that you mention it, why did you tell the media that you were going to renegotiate your contract early?"

"I didn't. My agent did." Anthony sat back on the sofa and took a long drink from his glass of water.

Faith gaped at him. "And he's still your agent?"

"If he backed off too soon, it would weaken my position when we negotiate at the end of the season." Anthony's scowl indicated he was far from happy with the position in which his agent had put him. It was also very sexy. "Training camp starts in two weeks and three days. The team doesn't need this distraction. *I* don't need this distraction."

"I think the team's already distracted." Faith's tone was dry. "Today's article quoted several of your teammates and other people from the franchise, criticizing you for renegotiating midcontract – all anonymously, of course."

"Renegotiating now wasn't my idea, either."

Faith's eyebrows jumped up her forehead. "Seriously, why is this guy still your agent?"

Anthony made a wry expression. "Because in the end, I agreed with him and so did my brother. I just hadn't expected things to go so wrong."

Faith was intrigued by the baller. The look in his eyes, the way his lips moved, his expressive features, the way he used his hands when he spoke. What had he been like as a little boy? Had he always had a basketball with him? It wasn't until this moment that Faith realized Anthony had been the inspiration for the comic strip hero in her head.

She gave herself a mental shake as she stood. "It's almost one o'clock. I'll make us some lunch, soup and sandwiches?" She'd originally planned for just the soup but she suspected that wouldn't be enough for a professional athlete.

"That'd be great. Thanks." Anthony rose as though to follow her. "I'll help."

Faith took his empty water glass, then led him to her kitchen. "Perhaps you can just keep me company. The kitchen isn't big enough for both of us." She refilled his glass with the water from the fridge, then returned it to him.

Cooking with Constance and Tiffany was one thing. Together, those two were still much smaller than a professional basketball player. Moving in such tight quarters with him would qualify as foreplay.

Faith pulled the remains of her homemade chicken and vegetable soup from the fridge. She opened the plastic storage container and poured enough for two servings into a pot, then placed it on the stove to boil. "You know if this is about making more money, that won't buy you happiness."

"I don't think anyone's ever told my brother that."

"Does your brother play professional basketball?"

"No."

Faith hadn't thought so. "But it was your brother and agent who talked you into renegotiating your contract early. What did you want?"

Anthony braced his shoulder against the kitchen threshold. "I wanted to wait until my contract was up."

"Are you sure you're following *your* dream and not theirs?"

"I'm sure." He didn't sound convinced.

Faith wasn't, either. "Just remember, this is your career. You should follow your instincts, even if it goes against what your agent and Paul recommend."

Anthony studied the floor as though he could see the future in the linoleum. "How will the team treat me after this coverage?"

Faith took the leftover rotisserie chicken she'd made for dinner the night before from the refrigerator. "It'll be uncomfortable for a while, but everything always works out in the end." Much like her career. She just wished she had a better handle on when to expect "the end."

"It's hard to say no to my brother." His voice was low and pensive. "I wouldn't be here if it wasn't for him."

Faith considered the tall, lean, well-muscled athlete. Finally, she dragged her gaze away and continued slicing chicken for their sandwiches.

"That's not true." She cleared her throat before speaking again. "He may have gotten you started, but your hard work and dedication got you to where you are today." She swung the knife to indicate the chiseled muscles of his arms and upper torso, and his long, sculpted legs. "Those muscles didn't magically appear. You work for them. You don't learn the Monarchs' game plan through osmosis. You study them."

Anthony seemed to ponder her words for a moment, then dropped the subject. He straightened from the doorway. "What can I do to help?"

Faith directed him to set the table and pour the juice. Minutes later, they were eating lunch in the little dining area. Their conversation was as fluid and fun during this meal as it had been during their dinner two nights previously. This time they shared stories of their families and childhood.

Anthony placed his empty soup bowl on top of the plate that once held his sandwich. He folded his arms on the table in front of him. His pose put those guns front and center. "Have you heard from your agent about how your comic strip is being received?"

"Not yet." Faith rescued herself from his penetrating stare. She could easily drown in those depths. "She's sent the proposal to several publishers and production companies."

"Great." Anthony's golden good lucks lit with pleasure. "Good luck. That's exciting."

Faith finished off the chicken vegetable soup, then set her bowl aside. "It will be – if anyone makes an offer."

"Your parents named you Faith, but you have so little of it." He made a tsking sound. "Matthew, chapter twenty-one, verse twenty-two, 'And all things whatsoever ye shall ask in prayer, believing, ye shall receive.'"

Faith flashed a grin. "Andrea told me your teammates nicknamed you Saint Anthony because you're always quoting passages from the bible. She also told me you hate being called that."

"I don't think they mean it as a compliment." Anthony's tone was dry. He collected the empty dishes and led the way into the kitchen.

"Probably not." Faith followed with the drink glasses and a chuckle. "But I've got a verse for you. Proverbs sixteen-nine, 'A man's heart deviseth his way: but the Lord directeth his steps.'"

"I like your style, Ms. Wilcox." He took the glasses from her and added them to the sink.

"My parents didn't name me Faith as a prank." She looked from Anthony to the sink. "What are you doing?"

"Washing the dishes." He paused before turning on the faucet. "Do you mind?"

"Twist my arm." Faith stepped back to the threshold, giving her guest more room.

"That was one of the best meals I've had in a long time. Thank you."

"Soup and sandwiches?" Faith gave him a dubious look. She enjoyed watching him clean the dishes, though. His movements were fluid and efficient. He wasn't a stranger to housework. She realized that she liked that in a man.

"*Homemade* soup and sandwiches." Their banter continued while Anthony completed the kitchen duty. When he was done, he stacked the dishes on the drain board and dried his hands on the kitchen towel. "Next time, the meal's on me at my place."

"Serge and Troy set the bar pretty high." Faith let him out of the kitchen. "I cooked a meal for them once and they repaid me with a steak dinner."

"I love a challenge." He stopped right in front of her. Another sexy smile curved his lips and brightened his eyes.

Faith felt his body heat. She should step back, but she didn't want to. Instead, she rose on her toes, giving him silent permission to kiss her. Anthony's touch was light, tentative. Faith could turn away at any time. She wrapped her arms around him, angling her head to invite him closer. Anthony took her into his arms and deepened their kiss. His tongue traced her lips coaxing her to part for him. Faith shivered as he slipped inside. Anthony tightened his embrace. His tongue tasted her, explored her, teased her. Faith did the same. His caresses stoked a slow heat inside of her that she'd been denying for some time. But she wasn't certain she was ready for it now.

Faith stepped back and opened her eyes. "This feels like something more than friendship."

Anthony searched her features. "Do you mind?"

"The timing isn't right for me." She caressed the side of his face. Her regret was physical.

He cupped her hand over his cheek. "When will it be?"

If only I knew.

CHAPTER 9

"I can tell there's something on your mind." Constance confronted Serge after they'd put Tiffany to nap in one of his guest bedrooms Saturday afternoon.

Serge loved that she could read him so well after only five months together. Still he dreaded telling her what had happened. It would only cause her pain and anger.

He shifted to face her on the soft loveseat, taking her hands in his. "I received a letter from Wade."

"My ex?" Constance frowned. Her Midwestern accent was more pronounced with her trepidation. "How did he get your address?"

"He sent it care of the Monarchs." Serge held on to her as he finished his news. "He offered to give up his parental rights for Tiff for a price."

"What?" Constance tore her hands from his and reared off the loveseat. "He's going to *sell* Tiff? How much?"

"Excuse me?" Serge was distracted by the fire in Constance's green eyes and the rose flush that stained her porcelain cheeks.

"How much money does he want for Tiff?" Constance balled her fists. Her voice strained for control.

When put that way, Wade's request was even more indecent. "Ten thousand dollars."

"Ten. Thousand. Dollars?" Constance's eyes stretched wide. She spun away from him. Serge couldn't tell whether it was in shock or disgust. Perhaps both.

Her sandals slapped the hardwood flooring as she circled the long, narrow living room. She passed the walnut wood and stone fireplace without a glance toward the framed photographs or impressionistic paintings surrounding her. With each stride, she vented her anger.

"He was *never* a father to Tiff. *Never.*" Constance spoke in harsh whispers as though afraid her daughter would hear her as she slept in a room down the hall. "He ignored her because she wasn't the boy he'd wanted. In the *five months* we've known you, you've spent more time with Tiff than Wade had in the first *three years* of her life."

Serge briefly squeezed his eyes shut against the pain in Constance's voice and the anguish in his heart. Wade was a horse's *ane*. "That's his loss."

But he didn't think Constance heard him. "Now he wants to make money off of her? The *hell* he will!"

Serge had expected her response, but he wanted to present his side. He had to call her name twice to get her attention. "I'd pay that price and more for the privilege to be Tiff's father."

His words elicited a look of surprise. Constance sounded dazed. "But we aren't married."

"We could be."

"You want to marry me?"

"Of course. And adopt Tiff."

"But we've only known each other a few months."

"Long enough."

Constance's wide eyes swept the living room as though searching for an escape route. Serge stood between her and his condo's only exit.

What was she afraid of?

She finally met his gaze. "Serge, being a parent is a big responsibility. You're enjoying Tiff now when you see her on the weekends or a couple of times a week, but she's not always this happy little girl. She's three, but she can be obstinate and defiant."

"Like her mother."

"I'm serious."

"So am I." Serge stood and crossed to her. He took her hands again. "Connie, I've been around enough children to know that every day is not Saturday. I love Tiff as I would my own child, and that's not just because she's yours and the mirror image of you. I love her because she's smart, fearless and funny."

"You love her now, but what about for the long term?" The concern in Constance's gaze chilled him. "Will you love her when she's a moody, argumentative, disrespectful teenager?"

Serge tried another smile. "If that happens, we'll remind each other why we love her, and talk each other out of driving her into the woods and leaving her there."

Constance didn't react to his joke. "What if you want children of your own?"

Serge dropped her hands and stepped back.

What is she trying to tell me? Whatever it was, it hurt.

"Connie, more children doesn't mean less love." He searched her troubled eyes. "What's worrying you?"

Constance shook her head. "I have to protect my daughter."

"From me?"

"From pain."

Each breath he took was like a blade in his throat. *Does she think I'm not good enough to be a parent to Tiff?* He was too afraid of the answer to ask the question.

"I wouldn't harm her. I love her as my own child." Serge turned away from the lingering doubt in Constance's eyes. He couldn't force her to believe him.

"I'm sorry, Serge, but everything I do affects her. I have to be sure I'm making the right decision."

"How do I convince you that *I'm* the right decision?"

"I need more time."

"All right." It wasn't the answer he'd wanted, but he'd accept it. For now. In the meantime, he'd take care of the loose ends.

***

At the age of nine, growing up outside of Atlanta, Faith had gazed at her ceiling in a bedroom more than twice the size of the one she slept in now. She'd fantasized about growing up to be a celebrated cartoonist in New York City.

Sunday morning, more than eighteen years later, Faith scowled up at the very different ceiling of the cramped bedroom in the apartment she shared with two other women and a three-year-old girl. The conditions were radically different from her childhood fantasies, nor had she dreamed she'd still be living this way more than five years after earning her fine arts degree.

For pity's sake, I'm still paying off my student loans.

The starry-eyed child she'd been hadn't imagined that her future roommates would put their lives on hold because they didn't believe she could fend for herself.

What a mess!

Faith grabbed her cell phone from the small stand beside her bed. She launched her Contacts directory and tapped the entry for her mother's landline. It rang several times before her mother answered. Just the sound of her voice filled Faith with comfort. She hugged the feeling to herself with both arms.

"Why do you sound like doomsday is just a couple of hours away?" JoyLynn Cambia Wilcox didn't participate in small talk. According to her, there wasn't enough time in the day. Even now, although Faith knew she had her mother's attention, JoyLynn's hands were probably doing three other tasks at once.

"I'm having a crisis of confidence."

"Did you go to Mass this morning?"

Faith ignored her mother's verbal eye roll. "Yes and although the sermon was lovely, it didn't really help."

JoyLynn grunted. "Obviously, you weren't listening hard enough. What's on your mind, baby?" The quiet hum of a washer played in the background. JoyLynn was doing laundry.

"The New York Horn won't pay me more for the BKLYN Crew." The despondency in her voice embarrassed her.

"You told me about those craven, penny-pinching Neanderthals." Her mother interrupted herself to quiet her two British Boxers. Their yips of greeting had turned into near-deafening demands for affection. "You also told me your agent was sending your work to other places. Has she heard anything?"

"No, she hasn't received any interest from publishers or production companies. I'm beginning to think she never will."

"There's my little gray cloud!" JoyLynn's tone dripped with sweet sarcasm. The clanking of metal and the rush of water indicated that JoyLynn was washing dishes while psychoanalyzing her daughter. Her mother: the ultimate multitasker. "I believe.

Your agent believes. What will it take for *you* to believe that you can succeed?"

"Success would help." Faith matched her mother's sarcasm.

"What do you call your contract with the Horn?"

"False hope." Faith pushed herself into a sitting position on her bed. "Real success would be the ability to support myself financially with my comic strips, but I can't. Now even my roommates have put their lives on hold because of me."

"What're you talking about?"

Faith gritted her teeth. She hadn't meant to blurt that out, but it was the reason she'd phoned home. "Andrea won't move in with her boyfriend because she's afraid Connie and I won't be able to afford the rent without her. Connie's also in a serious relationship. I bet she'll feel the same way eventually."

"What if she does?" JoyLynn didn't like even the hint of someone criticizing her "baby."

"Then she'd be right." Boy, did it pain Faith to admit that. "I can't manage any of these bills on my own, even with the combined income from the BKLYN Crew and the accounting firm."

Unless I give up luxuries like heat and food.

Water still flowed in the background from her mother's end of the line. How many dishes was her mother washing? Faith pictured her middle-aged mother, standing at the sink. The scarlet apron tied around her waist shouted, "Kiss the Cook!" in plain, bold white lettering across her chest. The window above the sink overlooked the cozy, ranch-styled home's backyard. It was early September, which was still considered summer. Were the leaves on the burning bushes turning red, yet?

"What's the worst-case scenario?"

Faith heard the mental shrug in her mother's voice. "I'll have to get one maybe two new roommates."

"Or you could come home. Focus on getting your accounting degree, if that's what you really want."

"But you want me to follow my dreams."

"Is it so wrong for a mother to want her daughter to be happy? It's what your father would've wanted, too."

"I know, Mom."

"Life's too short, baby." JoyLynn's tone was more persuasion than pressure. "Now's the time for you to take risks and chase dreams, while you're young and single. Why're you afraid of your own success?"

Her parents had given up their dreams to start a family. She wanted to fulfill her dreams in tribute to her parents and all they'd sacrificed so that she could be successful. Then, she wanted to start a family of her own.

"I'm afraid I'll never achieve it."

Her mother's sigh was overly long and unnecessarily dramatic. "That's your fear speaking. When will you stop listening to it?"

Faith didn't know if she ever could.

CHAPTER 10

"Serge wants to marry me." The words rushed out of Constance Sunday evening. She still felt as amazed as when Serge had made his declaration Saturday.

After dinner at home with Faith and Andrea, Constance had put Tiffany to bed in the room they shared. Then she'd joined the other women in their living room to wind down before the new work week. She sat beside Andrea on their lumpy sofa. Faith sprawled on their mismatched, battered armchair. But her announcement had brought both women to attention. They turned toward her like bullets. The adventure movie playing on their second-hand television was forgotten. They grinned at her, rushing to offer their congratulations.

"How did he propose?" Andrea was trembling with enthusiasm. Her rouge T-shirt was a warm splash of color against her powder blue baggy shorts.

"I can't believe you waited *a full day* before *saying* anything." Faith swung her long brown legs off the chair's arm, shifting to face the sofa. She planted her bare narrow feet on the vivid area rug.

"Well, he didn't actually propose. He said he wanted to marry me when I was ready." Sharing her concerns – large and small

– with people who had only her best interests at heart made a refreshing change. When she'd brought her troubles to her mother, it hadn't taken her long to realize Bettie Lee wasn't on her side.

Andrea nodded her approval. "Serge really cares about you."

Andrea's judgment gave Constance a warm glow, but she was still cautious. "How do you know?"

The reporter gave her an encouraging smile. "He knows you and Tiff have already been through several dramatic changes: a new home in an unfamiliar city, establishing a new routine with strangers, a new high-pressure career. He appreciates how stressful these changes have been for both of you."

Faith leaned forward on her seat. Her expression and tone were more than a little concerned. "Your divorce's final, Connie. What's really holding you back?"

Constance hesitated, worrying her hands together. "How would it look if I marry someone so soon after my divorce?"

"It would look as though you know your mind." Faith leaned back against her chair. Her electric green top and lemon yellow shorts glowed against the furniture's earth tones.

"What does it matter what anyone else thinks or says?" Andrea reached over to give Constance's hand a quick squeeze. "You know the truth. The only opinions that matter in this situation are yours, Tiff's and Serge's."

"It's Tiff's opinion that I'm worried about." Constance seized on Andrea's words. "I have to be a good role model for my daughter. The good Lord knows my mother wasn't any kind of a role model for me. When I told her Wade was abusing me, she told me it was his right."

Faith looked disgusted. "I still can't wrap my mind around how a woman could tell her daughter something like that. This isn't the dark ages. It's the twenty-first century."

"You stopped the cycle of violence, Connie." Andrea's sherry brown gaze held Constance's. "It's important to remember that."

"Andrea's right." Faith straightened on her chair, pushing back her cloud of dark hair. "You're the best role model Tiff could wish for. You're smart, fearless and loving."

Constance blinked back tears of gratitude. Not for the first time, she wished she'd known these supportive women before she'd married Wade, although she couldn't totally regret her failed marriage. It had given her Tiffany. "I don't want to go from one relationship to another. I don't want to have someone take care of me. I want to prove that I can take care of myself and Tiff."

Faith frowned. "You've already done that."

Constance shook her head violently. "I want to know for myself that I'm with Serge because I want him, not because I need him."

A ghost of a smile settled over Andrea's lips. "With love, need and want could be the same thing. Don't let that question drive you crazy. When you're ready to take your relationship with Serge to the next level, you'll know."

"At least Wade's out of your life." Faith breathed a sigh of relief.

"Serge got a letter from Wade." Constance was almost embarrassed to share this part. "He offered to sell his paternal rights to Serge for ten thousand dollars."

Stunned silence crashed into their tiny living room. The television commercial promoting breakfast cereal seemed absurdly loud.

Faith's stare was wide and unblinking. "What did Serge say?"

Constance pressed her fingertips against her closed eyes. "He wants to pay it."

"Is that wise?" Andrea's tone was tentative. "How do we know Wade won't keep asking for more money?"

"We don't." Constance dropped her hands and shrugged. "Between my mother and Wade, I feel like I'll never be free from my past."

Andrea leaned forward to hug Constance's shoulders. "Yes, you will."

Faith flashed a grin. "Now take your time and figure out what you want to do about it."

Constance had traveled full circle. Did her heart leap because she wanted Serge – or because she needed him?

***

What was Faith thinking?

Anthony observed Faith's meandering trail through his living room as he carried two glasses of iced tea to her Saturday afternoon. He caught up with her beside his ebony stereo system. "A penny for your thoughts."

"A penny?" Faith arched a brow as she accepted one of the glasses from him. In her lime green shorts and warm rose blouse, she'd brought summer into his home. "With inflation, it's a buck fifty now."

Anthony was skeptical. "Are your thoughts worth that much?"

"They must be worth a lot or you wouldn't be asking." Faith tossed him a saucy look as she wandered past him. The scent of citrus and roses trailed after her.

Anthony turned, tracking the movements of her long, slender figure around his black leather sofa, armchairs and loveseat, and the gray stone coffee table and matching light stands. He'd wanted to kiss her since he'd picked her up at her apartment and brought her back to his place for the lunch he'd promised her. He'd made salmon salad instead of steak.

It had been a week since they'd seen each other. Although they spoke on the phone every evening and texted each other throughout the day, he'd been anxious to see her. For the first time in years, he awoke more excited about a person than his training. Her texts made him smile. Their phone calls made him laugh out loud.

He liked having someone to wish goodnight. "What's your verdict?"

"Your home is beautiful." Faith turned to him. Teasing lights danced in her wide chocolate eyes. "Do all Monarchs employees use silver and black for their interior decorating or is it just the players?"

She'd baffled him. "What d'you mean?"

"At Connie's birthday party, didn't you notice that Serge also has a silver and black theme?" Faith spread her arms to encompass Anthony's living room. "Talk about taking your work home with you."

Her laughter was sexy over the phone lines. In person, it was as intoxicating as a rare liqueur. Anthony took a step toward her. "No, I hadn't noticed that. But now that you mention it, I think it may be all Monarchs employees." He'd been to Warrick Evans's house, the Monarchs forward, and Troy's condo a couple of times. He'd also been invited to Jaclyn's home for special team events, including the celebration of their NBA championship.

Faith sipped her iced tea, temporarily lifting the spell she was knowingly or unknowingly casting over him. "This is a striking room, but it needs a woman's touch. Serge's artwork adds color to his living room. Maybe you can do something like that."

Anthony had chosen the classic black and white photography of old Brooklyn that hung on his walls because he liked them.

Maybe Faith had a point about color, though. He'd think about that later. Tonight, he wanted to think about her.

He took another step closer, inclining his head toward her wrist. "Tell me about your Tinker Bell wristwatch. Was it a gift?" *If so, from whom?*

"Yes, from my parents." Faith glanced at the gold timepiece. "It's meant to encourage my dream. You know, wishing on a star? How are things progressing with your contract renegotiation?"

It was an awkward segue, but Anthony got the message: She didn't want to talk about her dreams anymore. He wasn't sure he wanted to talk about his contract. "Not well. A trade's on the table."

"Oh, no. What will you do if they trade you?"

"Paul doesn't think they will." He sipped his iced tea. He didn't want to leave Brooklyn. He didn't want to leave the Monarchs, either. And he was beginning to believe he didn't want to leave Faith.

"What do *you* think?"

"I think I want this to be over. Soon."

"It's so close to the start of the season." Faith searched his eyes. "Doesn't training camp start in a week?"

"A week and three days." Since both of her roommates were involved with the Monarchs organization in some capacity, it shouldn't surprise Anthony that Faith would be so familiar with the team's schedule. But it did.

"I hope this is resolved soon, too, and in your favor. The waiting game is murder." She offered him a smile but he could sense she was still troubled by his news. Was she reluctant to see him go?

He changed the subject. "Have you heard from your agent about your comic strip?"

"Not yet." Faith shook her head as she sipped more iced tea. "These things usually take a while. Have I told you that I hate the waiting game?"

Anthony grinned. "So do I."

He couldn't deny his need to kiss her any longer. Not when the memory of their last kiss haunted him morning, noon and night, and not when he saw the interest in her chocolate gaze. But her eyes also held a question. Was this wise? He didn't have an answer yet. Maybe after their curiosity was satisfied. He placed their glasses of iced tea on the mantel, then stepped closer to her. He lowered his head slowly, giving her a chance to change her mind. Anthony was relieved when she didn't stop him.

He pressed his lips lightly to hers, taking his time, testing their soft fullness. Stepping just a little bit closer, he pressed his mouth to her lips more firmly, separating them with his tongue and easing inside. It was a gentle foray into a tentative intimacy. Anthony remained attuned to her reaction, ready to step back at the slightest signal of unease, but hoping for just a few more moments. And a few moments more.

She was soft and so sweet, warm. His pulse picked up as his lips moved on hers. Exploring. Examining. Experiencing. He raised his arms from his sides and slid them around her, pressing her closer. His breath caught when her arms slid up his torso and settled onto his shoulders. Every muscle in his body shook. Or was that hers?

Anthony took their kiss deeper. His head spun. His breathing quickened. He couldn't get enough of her taste, her scent, her touch. Sensations were rocking him to his core.

And then she stepped away.

Faith looked as shaken as he felt. Her chocolate eyes were wide and burning into his. Her chest rose and fell with her rapid breaths. She gripped his arms as though she was desperate for him to keep her standing.

"I'm not going to apologize." He hadn't meant to say that.

"I wasn't going to ask you to."

Good. Her taste was still on his tongue. He was still touching her. Had she had the same reaction to that mind-blowing kiss that he'd had?

He struggled to gather his thoughts. "I'm not suggesting we rush into anything. We can take it slow."

Faith released her grip on his forearms and took a wobbly step backward. Then another. "I'm sorry, Tony. I can't."

His mind was still foggy, but that wasn't the only reason she didn't seem to be making sense. "Is there someone else?"

She gave him an are-you-kidding-me look. "I wouldn't be here with you if I was in a relationship with someone else."

"Then why not? I know you feel something between us, too."

Faith ran her hand over her thick, dark hair. "You've achieved your dream. You're a successful NBA player and you have a championship ring to prove it. I'm still chasing mine. A serious relationship would be a distraction for me."

Anthony captured her hand again. "I won't be a distraction, Faith. It's like you said. We're both dreamers. Whatever time, whatever space you need to go after your dream, I can respect that. Let me prove it to you."

"You're almost too good to be true." She arched an eyebrow.

"Just give me a chance. If things don't work out, then I'll understand."

She gave him a taste of the waiting game she hated so much. It was only a moment or two, but it felt like minutes. Finally, she smiled. "All right."

Anthony closed his eyes on a sigh. He felt like he'd beaten the buzzer to stay in the game. Now he could find out where these feelings for Faith Wilcox, accountant by day/cartoonist by night, were coming from and, more importantly, where they'd lead.

CHAPTER 11

"Could you repeat that?" Faith couldn't wrap her mind around her agent's words as they came through her cell phone. "Nothing? Not a single taker from any of the publishers or production companies you've contacted?"

She'd arrived fifteen minutes before she was expected at her desk Monday morning and called Lareeta on her cell phone from the first floor lobby of the building that housed her employer, Burnston & Banner, LLC. Had she known the news would be so devastating, she would have slept in.

"Not yet." Lareeta used the soothing but firm cadence of someone trying to talk another person away from the edge of hysteria.

Everything Faith was risking on her quest for success flashed across her mind. What was the point of pulling all-nighters to meet deadlines for projects that had such low returns? Or spending her vacation time and discretionary dollars on conferences and workshops when she'd rather visit her mother in Georgia? When would she have something to show for all of this?

Faith pulled her blazer more closely around her to ward off a sudden chill. The heels of her black pumps marked each step with an agitated click against the tiled flooring. "How many have you heard back from?"

"Of the publishing houses I've sent your series proposal to, three have responded so far." Lareeta sounded disappointed but resolute. "I know it's hard to hear that three have passed on your project, but it's been a week and I wanted to give you an update."

"I appreciate that." *What am I supposed to do now?*

"I've forwarded the publishing houses' emails to you for your records."

Faith gave a dry chuckle. "You say that as though I'm anxious to read more rejections. I've already got plenty of those to choose from."

"Two of the three publishers explained why the project wasn't right for them right now. You might get some helpful insight." Just under Lareeta's words, Faith heard the sound of metal tapping against porcelain. Her agent was fixing a cup of coffee. Faith could use a cup of tea.

The building lobby's black and white marbled tiles, and its black furnishings reminded Faith of Anthony's home.

Are the building's owners Monarchs fans?

Faith glanced at her wristwatch. It was almost ten minutes to nine o'clock. The groups of people making their way to the elevator banks grew larger the closer they got to the hour.

"I'll take a look at their feedback." Faith adjusted her bronze purse on her right shoulder. "Do you have any suggestions on how I could make the series more marketable?"

"You know I love your BKLYN Crew characters as though they were my own kids." Lareeta sighed. "Your proposal is still with seven other publishers. We'll find a good home for them."

"Suppose we don't?" The words hurt getting out.

"You're throwing in the towel already?" Lareeta seemed more disgusted than disappointed.

Faith blew a frustrated breath and settled her free hand on her hip. She kept her voice low. "I'd considered self-publishing my work, but that requires money I don't have. It's all I can do to pay my bills."

Faith forced a bright smile and friendly wave for a trio of coworkers who'd entered the lobby. They returned the greeting, but their curious looks foretold of numerous prying questions later. They could ask. They'd asked plenty of questions after Anthony's surprise visit to their offices. She'd give them the same answers she'd provided the last time: nothing.

"Faith, grow some patience." Lareeta's command brooked no argument. "If the seven other publishers still looking over your proposal don't give us an offer, there are still a lot more we can approach."

There was a lot riding on Faith's success: her dreams, her parents' dreams, her financial stability. And her future. She thought of Anthony. She was tired of putting her personal life on the shelf until her career took off. She was going to start believing in herself and living in the now.

Faith straightened from the cool lobby wall. "You're right, Lareeta. The BKLYN Crew will find a good home."

"And not just for the BKLYN Crew but for your other ideas, too. So strap in, girlfriend, we're in for a ride."

Faith felt a thrill of excitement. "I'm ready."

When she got to her desk, she'd find out if Anthony was still ready, too.

***

"I'm sorry your agent didn't have better news for you this week." Anthony sipped the freshly made iced tea Faith had prepared to accompany their dinner at her apartment Saturday evening. It was perfect; not too sweet, not too tart.

"I'm hoping one of the other publishers – or even a production company – will come through for me. Surely, it's time for some good news." Faith swallowed another forkful of the baked ziti she'd made for them.

Anthony tossed her a grin. "That's a much better attitude than the one you had last week." He forked up his pasta.

His gaze took in their place settings on the table in the apartment's little dining area. Faith's apartment was fragrant with the mouthwatering scents of her baked ziti and homemade bread. She'd also cut a tossed salad that was pure art with yellow, red, orange and green vegetables. He hadn't enjoyed a home cooked dinner made with this much care since his mother had died.

He could ask her to marry him based on this meal alone. That random thought sent his drink down the wrong windpipe, triggering a coughing jag.

"Are you all right?" Faith's chocolate brown eyes widened with concern.

"I'm fine." Anthony drank some more iced tea. This time, everything went where it was supposed to. "This meal is incredible. Thank you for cooking. The letters I'm getting from Monarchs fans about my contract renegotiation are a little...rough."

"I'm sorry." Her eyes were troubled.

His shrug was far more casual than he felt. "It was a risk. But fan reaction could make things awkward for you if we were seen together in public."

"Have your teammates said anything to you?" Faith gave Anthony a searching look.

Anthony paused. Faith had touched on the second most important issue affected by his agent's renegotiation. The fans were always his first concern. Their support of him and the team were important. He never wanted to let them down. A close second was his teammates' reactions. He didn't want to let them down, either.

"Training camp doesn't start for another three days, but some of the guys workout at the practice facility around the same time that I do. A few of them have made indirect comments that show they agree with the fans." Anthony sighed. "But most aren't saying anything. That's worse than outright criticism because I don't know where I stand with them."

"That's hard." Her gentle words captured his feelings exactly. "That tension's bound to affect your training camp."

"Yeah, Tuesday should be real interesting." Anthony's tone was dry as dust. Again, her concern was comforting and curious. Even Paul didn't express that much caring.

"But your teammates should know you better than to think that you'd put yourself ahead of the team."

"You'd think so, wouldn't you?" Anthony caught her eyes. "Once things die down, I'm going to fire my agent. What do you think?"

"What I think doesn't matter."

"I'd really like to know."

"Tony, at the end of the day, my opinion isn't important." Faith leaned forward, just missing the pasta sauce edging her plate. "Neither are the opinions of your fans and teammates, and even Paul and your agent. You're the one who has to live with the consequences of your actions and inactions, so your opinion's the only one that matters."

She had a point. He was the only one affected by his decisions - good, bad or indifferent. Everyone else could walk away – including Paul and Nyles. "In other words, I shouldn't have started down this path."

"Not if it wasn't the path you wanted to take." Faith sipped her iced tea. "But it's not too late to turn around."

It was amazing how much clearer his thoughts seemed after speaking with her. "I should've had this conversation with you weeks ago."

"Leave a nickel in the jar."

Her reference to the Peanuts character, Lucy, made him smile. "So tell me what made you change your attitude and become more optimistic about your career prospects."

"You did."

Surprised, Anthony looked up from his baked ziti. "Me? How?"

"We're both dreamers. You encouraged me to take the risk." Faith looked like he'd just given her a bouquet of rare roses.

Anthony liked the way that made him feel. "Then let's call it even."

He referred back to her Lucy comment about the nickel jar, but were there other dreams he could help her realize?

CHAPTER 12

"Maybe I should accept the offer." Faith stared at her home cooked grilled chicken salad.

A hectic morning had pushed her lunch to a much later hour. She held her fork in one hand and her cell phone in the other as she sat alone in the employee break room arguing in low tones with her agent. As usual.

Lareeta had emailed to Faith's personal account an offer from one of the publishing companies. To label the terms disappointing was overly diplomatic. The publisher's offer was better than what Faith was making now with the New York Horn but far below what she thought she deserved.

Am I being unrealistic?

"It's a crappy offer." Lareeta's unforgiving tone was almost drowned out by a commotion at the literary agency. She raised her voice. "If I weren't a consummate professional, I'd've told the publisher several creative things he could do with his terms. But, no. I forwarded it to you and I'm advising *you* to decline it. We can do better."

"Can we? It's been almost three weeks." Faith moved the lettuce around the plastic storage bowl in which she'd served her salad. She also turned up the volume on her cell phone to hear her agent better.

Additional background noises indicated her agent was having a late lunch as well. Faith imagined the older woman eating a deli sandwich and soup in front of her computer. The office window beside her framed an eleventh-floor view of Times Square. It was strange that they lived in the same city and spoke on the phone several times a month, but they only got together once a year.

"Have you put a time limit on these offers?" Lareeta's question didn't sound completely facetious. "Because if you have, I need to know."

"I can't put my life on hold indefinitely while I figure out whether I can support myself with my comic strips." An image of Anthony materialized in front of her. No, she wouldn't put her life on hold. "I think I should take this offer."

Lareeta's sigh was a mixture of impatience and empathy. It skimped on empathy. "I know it's your career, but this offer is garbage. Let's wait before we act on it. I'll tell the publisher you want some time to think it over."

"I don't want time to think it over." Faith was starting to panic again. She couldn't help it. She could already hear the train leaving the station without her. "We've already received three rejections."

"Three rejections and this lowball offer out of the *ten* submissions I sent. That leaves six other opportunities to get a decent contract." There was a loud crash, then the shouted conversations beyond Lareeta's office abruptly stopped. Her agent must have gotten up and slammed her door. The silence was golden.

"If the other companies were going to offer anything at all, they would've responded by now." Faith lowered her fork. "Have you heard from any production companies?"

"Not yet."

Another disappointment.

Faith paused as a coworker walked into the break room for a cup of coffee. The chubby male junior accountant gave her a curious look as he crossed to the coffee pots.

She gave him a bright smile, then lowered her voice to continue her debate with Lareeta. "I really think I should go ahead with this company."

"In publishing terms, a three-week wait time is nothing. Talk to me when you have a couple of months of waiting under your belt."

Faith was horrified. "I can't wait months."

"Then give me two weeks."

"Lareeta–"

"Just two weeks. Jeez. I'll tell the publisher we'll get back to him with an answer in two weeks." Her agent sighed again. "Seriously, sweetie, you don't want to seem too desperate."

But she was desperate. Desperation oozed from her pores. Her skin crawled with it. Desperation was becoming a close, personal friend.

Faith's coworker left the breakroom with a smile, a wave and a full cup of coffee.

She waved back before returning to her conversation. "All right. Two weeks from today, if we don't have any other offers from a publisher or a production company, I'll accept this one."

"Great. I'll call you back the morning of Tuesday, October tenth and we'll revisit this situation."

"Lareeta, no, I said–"

"Gotta go, sweetie. Enjoy the rest of your day."

The line went dead. Faith stared at her cell phone. She wasn't going through this debate with Lareeta again in two weeks. If there weren't any other takers, she was going to sign with this publisher. It wasn't the step forward she'd hoped to take with her career, but it was a start.

Where was the harm?

***

Anthony stripped the ball from Roger Harris, one of the hoopers who came off the bench. They were on opposite squads in this practice game on the Monarchs' opening day of training camp. Starters like Anthony wore silver T-shirts with black running shorts. Players who came off the bench were in black T-shirts and running shorts.

Anthony shouldered past Roger. He intended to take the length of the court and convert the turnover into two points.

"Pass!" DeMarcus shouted from the practice court's sideline.

Anthony turned a deaf ear to the coaching. He pivoted around Darius Williams, another player on the opposing practice squad. His attention was on the familiar slap-slap-slap of the rubber ball against the high-gloss hardwood court. He was going to prove that he was an important member of the team.

"Here!" Serge waved at him from the post. The big man was wide open for an easy layup.

But Anthony could handle this. His sneakers screeched against the court as he danced around the remaining blockers. His teammates shouted at him to just pass the ball to Serge. He ignored them. He didn't need any of them with their silent – and not-so-silent – condemnation of his decision to explore early contract renegotiations. He was isolated, shutout from the rest of the team. Fine. He could go it alone, on and off the court.

Anthony focused on the basket. He barely registered the defense that cleared his path. Warrick covered Darius. Vincent guarded Roger, but Jamal came out of nowhere. He slapped the ball away from Anthony, then sprinted down court.

Anthony spun, correcting his balance as he gave chase. He followed the slap-slap-slap of the ball and the high-pitched shrieking of Jamal's sneakers. He strained forward, reaching in to disrupt Jamal's dribble. The second-year player's kickback caught his foot. They dropped to the court in a tangle of limbs. Loose ball.

DeMarcus's whistle pierced the sudden silence. "Bring it in!" The second-year head coach sounded like he was chewing bricks.

Anthony pushed himself to his feet. He left Jamal to stand on his own.

"What's gotten into you?" Barron "Bling" Douglas, the veteran point guard and team co-captain, gave Anthony a concerned look.

Anthony didn't have an answer. He joined the other players in front of the bleachers while DeMarcus and assistant head coach Oscar Clemente eyed them in disgust.

"You look like you've never played together before." DeMarcus's irritation cracked across the practice court. "Do we have to relearn what it means to be a team?"

"Haven't you heard?" Jamal "Jam-On-It" Ward, the 20-year-old shooting guard, smoothed his cornrows. His taunting gaze zeroed in on Anthony. "We got a *star* now."

Anger goaded Anthony's already racing pulse. "Don't be a punk, Jamal."

"That's very low brow of you, Saint Anthony." Humor laced Vincent Jardine's words. The six-foot-eight-inch center planted his hands on his hips. "Have you forgotten the Gospel According to Saint Matthew, chapter five, verse five? 'Blessed are the meek for they shall inherit the earth.'"

Anthony struggled with his temper. "Proverbs seventeen, verse twenty-eight, 'Even a fool, when he holdeth his peace, is counted wise and he that shutteth his lips is esteemed a man of understanding.'"

"Guys, take that off the court." Warrick's annoyance rivaled DeMarcus's. "Coach's right. We have to be a team again."

"When have we ever been a team?" Barron seemed sincerely curious.

"Never." Vincent wiped sweat from his eyes. "Rick knows that better than most."

"You managed to be a team last season." Oscar's words dripped with contempt. "That's how we won the championship. You'd better find that team spirit again or you'll be watching the finals on T.V."

DeMarcus massaged the back of his neck. "Look, this isn't the first time we've had to deal with controversy and gossip. If you can't separate what you read in the papers from what we're trying to do on the court, stop reading the sports section. There's plenty of other news in the papers."

Jamal slid another look toward Anthony. "But, Coach, how are we supposed to know when there's a snake in our group?"

DeMarcus stared down each player. One by one, they looked away. "Those of you who want to spend the rest of practice discussing Tony's contract step forward."

Jamal was the first to move. Anthony's heart sank. It dropped even farther when Roger and two other players followed. He looked to DeMarcus. Would he demand that Anthony give up his renegotiation? Should he allow his coach to dictate his career?

DeMarcus considered the players in front of him. "You four will spend the preseason on the bench. Make sure you renew your subscription to the Horn. You'll need something to read."

He turned to the other players. "The rest of you, I expect you to focus on the championship. Back to the court."

Anthony addressed his coach. "Thank you."

DeMarcus scowled at him. "This isn't about you. It's about the ring. I don't care what you do about your contract as long as you don't lose sight of the championship." DeMarcus gave him his back.

Anthony glanced over his shoulder and witnessed the fury of the group who'd stepped forward. He'd dealt with tension and resentment from other players before. This was more than that. He'd become a polarizing figure on the team. What did this signal for the Monarchs' season?

CHAPTER 13

"Saint, wait up." Barron's voice followed Anthony from the Monarchs' locker room late Tuesday afternoon.

He hated that nickname. Anthony turned, swallowing a sigh as he waited for the former team captain. "What's up, Barron?"

"Look, man, this may not be my place." Barron hooked an arm around Anthony's shoulders and set a slow pace down the hallway to the building's exit. "I don't know what all's going on with your contract but can I give you some advice?"

Anthony stopped in his tracks. "It would make a refreshing change from the whispers behind my back."

Years ago, he'd accepted that the players would never be friends outside of the arena. They barely spoke to each other on the court. A classic example of the dysfunction that burdened the team was the way the players – himself included – had treated Warrick Evans when the media were feasting on his failing marriage. Instead of supporting him during that painful time, they'd piled on even more pressure.

Barron dropped his arm and paced beside Anthony. "Look, man, last year, I felt like you do now, you know? I was the captain. I felt that *I* should be the star of the team. I'd been on the team longer than anyone but Rick, who I thought was washed up, but I was wrong. Boy, was I wrong."

Anthony winced. His agent's proposal sounded worse coming from a teammate he respected. "None of that was my idea."

"The idea may not have come from you, but you didn't dismiss it when someone else brought it up." Barron's hold on Anthony's gaze forced him to see the truth of those words.

Accountability was often hard to swallow. "You're right."

They continued down the wide tan hallway toward the exit. Natural light flowed through the glass front façade, flooding the space. Their gym shoes squeaked against the waxed tiled flooring. The black and silver Brooklyn Monarchs logo was emblazoned on the wall to the right.

Several trainers and teammates occupied the lounge area on the left. A few played pool at one of the tables. Another pair used the Ping-Pong table. A group sprawled on the comfortable sofas and stylish armchairs that sported the franchise logo and team colors while they watched a sporting event on the large, high-definition television mounted to the ceiling. They were snacking from some of the healthy selections they'd probably chosen from the nearby vending machines.

In the conversation area on the other side of the vending machines, Serge sat with Warrick and DeMarcus. The trio leaned forward on the overstuffed black and silver patterned chairs. They looked up briefly to return Barron's and Anthony's silent salutes.

Anthony pushed through the glass front doors, nodding at the security guards standing duty there. Fall had come to Brooklyn almost a week ago. He smelled it in the air around him. He felt it in the crisper-than-usual breeze that blew off the nearby marina and worked its way into his pale gray cotton jersey. From this distance, he could just make out the tops of the slender black lamp posts along the fence that lined the boardwalk. Between the marina and the practice facility stood the Empire Arena, home of the Brooklyn Monarchs since 1956.

Barron's counsel interrupted his thoughts. "Trying to be the star of the Monarchs put a lot of pressure on me."

Everyone in Brooklyn knew about the pressure Barron had been under last season. The burden had been so great that Barron had started drinking. A lot. In the middle of the NBA season, Jaclyn and DeMarcus had put Barron on the injured reserve list while he checked himself into an alcoholism recovery program. He'd also granted an interview with Andrea for her newspaper, hoping to help others who were struggling with personal demons.

Anthony placed a supportive hand on Barron's shoulder. "The recovery program was a hard decision for you, but it was the right one."

"I'm glad I did it." Barron took a deep breath. "While I was in that program, I had a lot of time to think about decisions that I'd made. You know what I realized?"

"What?"

"I was a fool. I was trying to be the star of a team that isn't designed to have one. Coach told me that, but I wasn't trying to hear it."

This was a revelation for Anthony as well. "You're right. When Coach joined the franchise last season, he changed our game."

"He made all of us stars." Barron faced Anthony. "So, Saint, if you want to be a Monarch, this is your home. But if you want to be a star, you'll have to find another team."

His brother thought Anthony should be the team's star, but that wasn't the way DeMarcus ran his team. As Faith had pointed out, the only opinion that mattered was Anthony's. So what was his game plan? Would he continue to placate Paul or call his own plays?

***

"Why won't she marry me?" For Serge, weeks of frustration over his stalled relationship with Constance had boiled over. Serge had become "that guy," the lovesick suitor, seeking advice and guidance from those who'd been there before him, specifically veteran teammate, Warrick Evans.

Serge sat with Warrick and their coach, DeMarcus, in the conversation area on the first floor of the Brooklyn Monarchs' practice facility late Tuesday afternoon. They'd officially finished the opening day of training camp. He'd sought Warrick's counsel because the player was happily married. DeMarcus, who was engaged to Jaclyn, the franchise's owner, had joined them.

The chairs were arranged in a close circle. Seated to Serge's right, Warrick gave an incredulous laugh. "You've only known Connie for five months."

The Monarchs' starting forward had changed into a navy IZOD short-sleeved shirt, baggy cream shorts and sneakers. He looked like he'd just strolled through a park instead of participating in a grueling four-hour team practice.

"I've wanted to marry her since the first week we met." Serge scowled at the tan half wall that separated the conversation area from the lounge where the television blared the day's sports news. "I'm in love with her and I know she loves me."

Warrick's bright brown eyes twinkled with good humor. "How do you know she's in love with you?"

Serge's blue eyes widened with surprise. "Why else would she allow me to spend so much time with her and her daughter?"

Serge looked up as Anthony and Barron walked past on their way out of the facility. They were similarly dressed in dark shirts, blue jeans and gym shoes. He raised a hand to acknowledge their silent salutes.

"I understand your impatience, Serge." DeMarcus turned back to their conversation after also waving goodbye to the two players. "I proposed to Jack in April. She still hasn't picked a wedding date. It's frustrating."

DeMarcus and Jaclyn's attraction had been tangible from the beginning. The couple was very much in love. The only thing holding up the ceremony was Jaclyn's reluctance to identify a date. It was cruel.

Serge gave his head coach a baffled look. "Why won't she set a date?"

"I don't know." DeMarcus shrugged his broad shoulders beneath his gray Monarchs T-shirt. The team's logo was emblazoned across his chest. "Every time I ask her, she says she needs to sit down with the preseason, regular season and postseason schedules, and pick the best time to plan the wedding and the best day to have the ceremony. How long would that take, five minutes? I've been waiting five months."

Serge saw his own frustration in the agitated lights burning in DeMarcus's coal black eyes.

"Why don't *you* pick the date?" Warrick asked.

Serge eyed the other man suspiciously. Did he find their turmoil amusing?

"I have. She said she'll consider it." DeMarcus ran a large hand over his close-cropped hair. "The only thing keeping me sane is that I know she loves me. I just can't understand why she won't set a date."

"I want Connie, Tiff and me to be a family." Serge turned to Warrick. "How did you convince Mary to marry you?"

Warrick was married to Dr. Marilyn Devry-Evans, a successful obstetrician/gynecologist. Their union had hit a rocky spot during the postseason but they'd hung on through the fire and their love had emerged even stronger.

"Gentlemen, love is like basketball." Warrick split a look between Serge and DeMarcus. "Timing is everything. Be patient with Connie, Serge. You don't want her to think that she *needs* to be with you. You want her to *want* you to be a part of their lives."

"How long will that take?" Serge had hoped his teammate would have some magic words he could use to persuade Constance to marry him.

"It'll take as long as it takes." Warrick shrugged. "Put yourself in Connie's place. You don't want her to feel that you're rushing her, do you?"

"Of course not." Serge shook his head adamantly.

Warrick continued. "She's finally gotten out of one controlling relationship. You don't want her to feel as though she's going into another one."

"Definitely not." Serge swept his hand decisively.

"Good." Warrick gave a nod of approval. "Be patient. She'll let you know when she's ready to take your relationship to the next level."

Serge felt better even though he wasn't any closer to convincing Constance to marry him. She and Tiffany were in his life and safe from Wade. That's what mattered for now. When the time was right, they'd be a family, whole together. "Thanks, Rick."

Warrick leaned forward to pat his shoulder. "Anytime, man."

DeMarcus looked from Serge to Warrick. "Now how do I translate this camaraderie to the court?"

Warrick ran a hand over his clean-shaven head. "I wish I could tell you, Coach."

"Then tell me this." DeMarcus addressed Warrick. "What about getting Jack to set a date? Do I just need to be patient and give her more time?"

"No, you need to get on that." Warrick's voice was firm. "Jackie and I have been friends for years. I love her like a sister."

"I know." DeMarcus's eyebrows knitted with concern.

"She's an amazing basketball player, a smart lawyer and a brilliant businesswoman." Warrick shifted forward on his seat. "But in her personal life, she's a *horrible* procrastinator. She used to drive her grandfather nuts. Don't let her procrastinate. Tell her that if she doesn't plan the wedding, you will. That should get her moving."

"All right." DeMarcus looked like a man ready for battle.

Serge had an uncomfortable foreboding. The struggle wouldn't be easy. "I don't envy you, Coach."

"That makes two of us." DeMarcus's voice was dry.

"Three," Warrick added.

Serge stood. "But our ladies are worth it."

He raised a hand in farewell as he strode toward the exit. His steps were much lighter than when he'd walked in. He was happy to wait for Constance and Tiffany. But that didn't mean he couldn't spend the time convincing Constance why she wanted him to be her number one pick.

CHAPTER 14

"I've got bad news." Nyles made his announcement Wednesday evening when he called Anthony at the end of the second day of training camp.

"You mean *more* bad news?" *Why haven't I fired this guy yet?* The reason was Paul.

Anthony hit the Mute button on his television's remote control. He'd settled onto his favorite overstuffed armchair in his living room after dinner. His cooking had made him pine for Faith even more. When his cell phone had rung, he'd hoped she'd be on the other end. Imagine his disappointment at the sound of Nyles's voice. And now his agent was telling him that he wasn't going to enjoy this conversation. Willpower kept him from disconnecting the call.

How could the situation get worse? Fan outrage was dying down, but as the sports blogs could attest, there was still enough hostility toward him to keep Anthony from socializing in public for a while longer. Maybe he should stop reading the blogs.

"I just got off the phone with Jackie Jones." Nyles cleared his throat. "I've tried everything that I could think of but she refuses to entertain renegotiations for your contract until closer to the end of this season when it's due to expire."

Anthony rolled his eyes in frustration. "I warned you this would happen."

"I know. I'm sorry." There was a tapping on the other end of the line as though Nyles was hitting a pen against his desk. The young man must be more agitated by his conversation with Jaclyn than he was letting on.

Anthony wasn't surprised. Jaclyn had successfully navigated the many duplicitous schemes her former partner, Gerald Bimm, had put into play against her. Anthony couldn't imagine a more vicious adversary. In comparison, dealing with Nyles would be like driving over a pot hole.

"I'm glad the renegotiating's over." His measure of relief surprised him.

"Well, it's not...exactly." Nyles's voice was so low Anthony wasn't sure he'd spoken.

He braced himself. "What does that mean?"

"Jackie doesn't want to stand in the way of your making more money. She's offered to add you to a trade deal she's putting together to get Marlon Burress from the Miami Waves."

Anthony went cold. "She wants to trade me to the Waves?"

"She won't really trade you, Sai...Tony." Nyles's voice spewed panic. "You're too valuable to the team. She's bluffing to scare us off of asking for more money."

"Jackie doesn't waste her time with bluffs." Anthony pushed himself from his armchair and marched barefoot to his kitchen. He needed a drink.

Anthony hadn't known Jaclyn long. For the majority of his Monarchs career, he'd played for Jaclyn's grandfather, Franklin Jones. The Joneses were a lot alike, though. Her grandfather hadn't wasted time with bluffs, either.

"So what if she's not bluffing? Miami is a great city. Would it really be so bad to be traded?"

"Yes." Anthony grabbed a glass from one of the blonde wood cabinets above his sink and filled it with filtered water from his faucet. "I told you that the first time you mentioned a trade. No. Trade."

Sure, Miami was a rocking city. There was a lot going on there. But it wasn't home. There was a lot going on in Brooklyn, too. He was born and raised here. He had lifelong friends here. His brother was here.

Faith.

Nyles was still talking. "This could be a golden opportunity for you. It could give you the chance you've been waiting for to raise your professional profile to the next level. You can be a star in Miami." Nyles's words sped up as though speaking faster would change Anthony's mind.

It wouldn't.

Anthony took a long drink of the cold water. "I'm staying with the Monarchs. Any talk of trading me to Miami or anywhere else is a nonstarter. Understand?"

Nyles drew an audible breath. "Yes, of course. But a trade would mean more money for you."

"And for you."

"I'm on your side, Sai...Tony. Besides Jackie's not going to trade you. This is probably just talk."

"It's a dangerous game of chicken, and I'm not going to play." Anthony paced his kitchen. The white marble tile was cool beneath his bare feet.

"I think that your brother would want you to at least consider this opportunity. It could be a win-win, if you give it a chance."

The muscles in the back of Anthony's neck tightened. "Have you spoken with Paul?"

"What? I...You told me not to."

He was lying. Anthony ran a hand over his close-cropped hair. It was time to find new representation. It was time to call his own game plan.

In the meantime, Nyles would fix the mess he'd made under the guise of "contract renegotiations." "Call Jackie first thing in the morning – *first thing* – and tell her that I *don't* want to be traded to another team. Tell her that I'm staying with the Monarchs. These renegotiations end today."

"Well, sure, Saint...I mean, Tony." Nyles paused. "Do you want to talk to your brother first?"

"No, and neither do you. Paul doesn't have a stake in this. I built my career with my own hard work." And he had Faith to thank for helping him to realize that.

Finding a new agent wasn't the only change he needed to make. He needed to have a heart-to-heart with his big brother.

***

"I have a bone to pick with you, little girl." Constance's mother sounded like she was chewing glass.

How much would it cost to get caller identification?

The idea came to Constance as soon as she heard Bettie Lee Maddox's voice on the other end of her apartment's telephone landline Wednesday evening. The term little girl wasn't an endearment on Bettie Lee's tongue. It was meant to make her feel inadequate.

"What's on your mind, mother?" Constance sent her roommates an apologetic look as she carried the cordless telephone into her bedroom. Faith and Andrea looked concerned. Tiffany remained focused on the dishes she was carrying to the kitchen.

They'd just finished dinner. Wednesday was the night they stayed in to have dinner and watch television together. Faith usually cooked while Andrea, Constance and Tiffany cleaned up before retiring to their tiny living room. Her roommates understood that she'd rather help with kitchen duty than speak with her mother.

"Your boyfriend sent Wade ten thousand dollars." Bettie Lee sounded as though Constance had committed an unforgiveable act of betrayal.

Constance's knees went out. She dropped to her bed in shock. Had Serge bought Wade's parental rights? She'd asked him not to do that.

She couldn't let her mother see how much this news disturbed her. Constance took a slow even breath, inhaling Tiffany's baby powder scent. "Is that the reason for your call? If so, I need to get Tiff ready for bed."

Bettie Lee gasped. "Livin' in New York City has destroyed your manners, little girl."

More like I'd finally found my backbone in the concrete jungle.

But she didn't want to push it. After all, Bettie Lee was her mother. "What can I do for you?"

Bettie Lee paused. There was a clicking sound and another pause. "You can explain why your boyfriend saw fit to send your *ex-husband* money before your *mother* saw even one red cent."

Constance tightened her grip on the telephone's receiver. She wasn't going to get into that. There were too many minefields on that path. "What do you need money for?"

"I'm your mother. How dare you even *ask* me that?" Bettie Lee took a deep breath. Her mother was smoking. Cigarettes and beer were probably on the night's dinner menu.

Constance squeezed her eyes shut, straining to hold on to her patience. "Why do you need money, mother?"

"Why do I have to have a reason? Can't I just wanna buy nice things for myself? I'm sure *you* have nice things."

Constance surveyed the little bedroom she shared with her three-year-old daughter. It stored only the bare necessities: the full-sized bed they shared, a nightstand with a lamp and alarm clock, a chest of drawers, and a mirror on the other side of the small closet door. "I make good money, but it's not enough to afford the types of things you're referring to. New York is expensive, and I have a daughter to care for."

Bettie Lee cackled without humor. "You must think I'm stupid. I know you're not buyin' those nice things for yourself. Your man's buyin' 'em for you. That's the way it works."

Constance smiled. Serge had indeed bought Tiffany and her a lot of nice things: flowers, tickets to children's movies, picnics and trips to the zoo. But those weren't the "nice things" to which Bettie Lee was referring.

Constance frowned. "Listen, mother, I'll send you some money once I'm more settled."

"Why can't your boyfriend send me money now like he did for Wade?" Her mother's response was sharp with disappointment.

"My boyfriend's name is Serge." Constance lost the battle for her patience. "And he won't send you money because you're not his mother. For God's sake, mother–"

"Don't take the Lord's name in vain with me, little girl."

"–Serge doesn't even know you."

"He knows *you*."

"And I will *not* ask him for money."

"Not even for your mama?"

"Not even for you. My relationship with Serge isn't about what he can give me or my family."

"Well, Connie Lynn, I'm disappointed in you."

No more disappointed than I am in you. "I'll send you money when I'm able, but I won't if you're going to be unreasonable."

"*Unreasonable–*"

"Mother." Constance inserted a warning note in the word.

There was a short pause. Constance sensed Bettie Lee pouting in that silence.

"Fine." Bettie Lee snapped her acquiescence before disconnecting the call.

Not surprisingly, Constance wasn't motivated to rush out and write Bettie Lee a check, but she was going to ask Serge about the money he'd sent to Wade – once she calmed down.

***

"They tradin' you for Marlon Burress?" Jamal's words came from behind Anthony in the hallway Thursday afternoon. He was leaving the practice facility after the third day of training camp.

Anthony turned to the second-year NBA player. The mockery on the twenty-year-old point guard's thin face didn't get to him anymore. The kid always looked like that.

"I'm not any part of a trade deal." He'd confirmed that with his agent first thing this morning. Right before he fired him.

Anthony glanced at his watch. Did Paul's urgency to speak with him after practice this afternoon have anything to do with the trade talks?

Jamal looked like a character from Faith's BKLYN Crew comic strip. He'd changed into a pair of baggy dark blue jeans and an oversized white T-shirt. The outfit looked like he'd borrowed the clothes from a friend who was three times his weight and half-a-foot taller. The strap of his red gym bag crossed his chest from his right shoulder. His thick gold chain held his self-identified nickname, Jam-On-It, above his abdomen. Anthony refused to use that moniker. It was worse than the nickname the team had given him.

The younger man stopped an arm's length away. "Is the honey you're dating the reason you're up here trying to renegotiate your contract early?"

"Faith has nothing to do with my contract." What kind of women did Jamal spend time with? It had never occurred to Anthony to discuss the terms of his contracts with the women he dated and none of them had ever asked. "I've got to go. I have an appointment."

Anthony inclined his head toward the security guards at the front exit. He pushed through the door, then turned toward the section of the parking lot in which he'd left his silver Lexus.

Jamal followed him. "So why'd you bag your talks, then?"

"Why're you so curious about my contract?" Anthony stopped to study Jamal. They weren't friends. They weren't even friendly. So why was the second-year player asking these personal questions?

"It's kinda whack, you know?" Jamal shrugged his broad shoulders under his oversized T-shirt. "You're dating this honey, and you and your contract are all over the news. You know? The next minute, the media says you dropped your renegotiations. That's it. It's over. It's gotta be 'bout the honey. She dump you?"

"It's not about Faith." Anthony adjusted the black nylon gym bag on his shoulder. "Jackie wasn't going to give me more money, but she said if I wanted a richer contract, she'd include me in a trade deal. I don't want to be traded."

Jamal gaped at him. "So you're gonna give up a fat contract for some honey? That's cray."

Anthony turned to leave. "Believe what you want."

"There're honeys at every arena, man." Jamal put a delaying hand on Anthony's shoulder. "Besides, you don't think it's whack that all three of those roomies are getting with Monarchs?"

Anthony removed Jamal's hand from his shoulder. "Andrea covered the Monarchs for years for her newspaper. That's how she and Troy met. Connie works with us, which is how she met Serge. And I met Faith through Troy and Serge."

"You sure about that, man?" Jamal gave him a knowing look.

Anthony drew a long calming breath, inhaling the tangy scent of fall leaves. It had been a long four-hour practice. DeMarcus had drilled them as though he was punishing them for a losing season when they'd actually beaten the odds to win their franchise's first NBA championship. If Anthony hadn't kept in top shape during the offseason, he'd be crawling across the parking lot right now.

"Make your point, Jamal." Anthony pulled the keys to his car from his black warmup pants, signaling that he was this close to walking away.

"OK. Those three honeys, dating three of *us*?" He gave Anthony a pitying look. "Those women planned it and ya'll three are too stupid to see it."

Anthony felt like he was looking at a stranger. "How long have you been paranoid?"

"Check it." Jamal shoved his hands into the pockets of heaven-knows-whose-pants he'd borrowed. "Why did you bag your renegotiation? You want more Benjamins and you want to be a star. Well, you can't get there from here, old man. You need to step out. Instead, you're gonna stay here and be some punk for some honey."

The "old man" reference wasn't appreciated, especially since every bone in his body hurt. Anthony turned to walk away. "I'm staying in Brooklyn because Brooklyn's my home."

"You're staying because you're blinded by the honey." Jamal kept pace beside him. The hem of the warmup pants dragged along the sidewalk like a train on a nontraditional wedding gown. "She wants you to stay in Brooklyn so that she could play house with you."

"You don't even know Faith. How can you judge her?" At one time, Anthony had done the same thing. It had been one of the most critical mistakes he'd ever made.

"Honeys try to make you think you need them. Giving you advice, telling you what you should do and how you should do it."

"Thanks for the warning."

"They'll memorize your schedule so that they know where you'll be and when better than you do."

Faith often quoted the Monarchs' schedule to him. He'd thought that was odd. "I'll keep that in mind."

"She'll use that Jedi mind trick on you, saying you need a 'woman's touch' or your place does. That's code for, 'Let me move in, rent free.'"

Anthony hesitated as he heard similar words in Faith's voice. But that was ridiculous. Faith wasn't like that. "I pity you, Jamal. You have such little respect for women. They aren't all manipulative or untrustworthy."

"That's what *you* think."

"You don't have much regard for men, either, if you think we're all gullible." Anthony looked both ways before crossing into the parking lot to find his car.

Jamal continued to dog his steps. "She's playing you, man. I can tell."

What crap. "How can you tell?"

"Think about it. Troy's going to ask Andrea to marry him, then Serge's going to ask Connie. Faith'll be all alone. She's setting you up, man. You'd better get woke."

"Jamal, go home." Anthony continued toward his car.

The young player had just turned twenty, but he had the maturity of an eight-year-old. This wasn't someone from whom a thinking person would take life advice.

Then why couldn't he get the kid's words out of his head?

CHAPTER 15

Late Thursday afternoon, Constance looked up from her desk outside of Troy's office on the Monarchs' executive floor in the Empire Arena. Serge smiled as he approached her. She'd known he'd come. He always stopped by after training camp.

Constance rose and circled her solid walnut wood desk to meet him halfway. She kept her voice low. "We have to talk."

She smoothed the skirt of her brick red coatdress as she led Serge to a quiet corner of the hallway away from the elevators. Her cream pumps tapped against the elegant silver and black tile. Serge's sneakers were silent behind her.

Constance squared her shoulders, then turned to face the blonde giant. He was a distraction in tight blue jeans and faded gray T-shirt that clung to his chest like a second skin. His golden hair was gathered into a stubby ponytail at the nape of his neck. Constance took a deep, steadying breath. The hallway smelled like wood polish and lavender freshener.

"You sent Wade a check for ten thousand dollars." She made the words a statement, not a question. What was the point? They both knew it was true.

The confusion in Serge's sapphire eyes cleared. It was replaced by wariness. "Did he tell you?"

"Never mind how I found out." Constance set her fists on her hips and scowled up at the professional athlete. "I specifically asked you not to do that. I didn't want you to buy parental rights for my daughter."

Serge's expression cooled. His lips tightened. "Do you think I'm not good enough to be a parent to Tiff?"

Constance rocked backward. "Where did you get that idea?"

Serge leaned toward her and lowered his voice. "Why else wouldn't you want me to have these rights if it's not because you don't think I could be a father to her? *Je ne suis un bete.*"

"I have to learn French."

Serge stepped back and took a breath. He crossed his arms over his chest. "I said I'm not a fool."

This was the first time he'd ever been angry with her. By rights, Constance should have been frightened or at least nervous. He was bigger than Wade, and every time Wade had even looked at her wrong, she'd thought she'd faint. But she wasn't afraid of this angry giant. She knew how gentle he was.

Constance closed the gap between them and rested her hand on his upper arm. The muscles beneath her fingertips were taut. Something flickered in his blue eyes before his scowl returned. It was as though for a moment, he forgot to be angry.

"You misunderstood my objection. I think you'll be a wonderful father and I know Tiff loves you."

Serge didn't appear satisfied. "Then why did you say I'd treat her differently if we have other children?"

"Raising a child is a huge responsibility. I can't expect you to raise someone else's."

"But I don't think of her as someone else's. I want her to be mine."

Stubborn man.

Constance dropped her hand from his arm and covered her face in frustration. "Why are we even having this conversation?"

"Because we should agree on something as important as parenting before we get married."

Constance's hands fell. She looked to Serge. His blue eyes challenged her. He spoke as though there wasn't a doubt in his mind that they were going to get married. It was just a matter of when.

She wanted to be swept away in a happily-ever-after with him, but there were so many things she had to accomplish first. "We've only known each other a few months."

"Five months, one week and five days."

Oh, dear heavens. "My divorce was only final a couple of weeks ago."

"Exactly three weeks ago today."

OK, she was impressed. "Serge, there're so many things that I still have to accomplish."

"I know that you want to prove that you're strong enough to make it on your own." Serge cupped her shoulders with his large palms. "You've already done that. Everything you've done since you left Wade, you've done on your own. I'm so impressed by you. But, Connie, you don't have to go it alone anymore. I'm right here and I want to help."

His words healed her. They made her feel whole, something she'd never felt before. "I want to get my degree."

"And I want to help you." Serge's words sped up with excitement. "I'll help you study for tests. I'll keep Tiff entertained while you do your homework. You can do these things on your own, but why should you have to when I want to be a part of your life."

Am I dreaming? "You make it sound so easy."

"Why does it have to be hard?" He gave her a quizzical smile.

"We don't have to get a minister tonight or even tomorrow. If next week's still too soon, I'm willing to wait."

He wanted to marry her. This honorable, loving, gentle man wanted to build a life with her and her daughter.

Was her grin as idiotic as she felt? "We'll have a long engagement."

Serge swept her off her feet and pulled her close for a deep kiss. His arms wrapped around her, holding her tightly to him. Constance twined her arms around his neck and kissed him back. Her body melted against him.

Finally, Serge returned her to her feet. "A long engagement, but not too long."

"I know." Constance raised her hand to cup the side of his beautiful face. "We're chasing more than a championship this season."

CHAPTER 16

"Did that woman you're dating convince you to end your contract renegotiations?" Paul looked and sounded irritated as he led Anthony into his great room later that Thursday afternoon. The gray wall-to-wall carpeting needed to be vacuumed or cleaned – or both.

Why was everyone accusing Faith of meddling in my professional career?

Anthony had come to Paul's house straight from practice. He was tired and impatient. "Faith doesn't have anything to do with my contract – and neither should you."

"What did you say to me?" Paul came to an abrupt stop. He turned toward the room's entrance where Anthony stood with his hands in his pockets.

"What's made you so hands-on with my career all of a sudden?" Anthony looked at his brother in bewilderment. "When I first entered the league, you left my career decisions to me and my agent. Now that I have a championship ring, suddenly you know what I need and when for my career better than I do. What makes you think you have that right?"

"You wouldn't even *be* in the league if it wasn't for me." Paul rose up on his bare toes. "You wouldn't have that *ring* without me."

Anthony turned away to pace the great room. He'd known Paul considered himself responsible for Anthony's success. He blamed himself for that. Over the years, he'd credited Paul with nurturing his love for the game and helping him to hone his skills. Perhaps, as Faith had suggested, he'd given his brother too much credit.

"You started me on this course and I'm grateful for that." Anthony met his brother's gaze. "But I'm the one doing the work necessary to stay in the league."

Paul's eyes widened in shock. "I taught you everything you know about the game."

Faith's words echoed in Anthony's head. "I'm the one in the gym. I'm the one studying the game film and the playbook. This is my career. My dream. Not yours. You got me started, Paul, but I'm the one who earned the ring."

"I know what this is." Paul stepped back, adding to the distance between them. "This is her, turning you against me."

"No, she's not."

What could he say to make his brother understand that this was about their relationship and Anthony's need to go back to making his own shots about his career?

His eyes swept the room in the home he'd helped his brother buy. When was the last time Paul had dusted? He felt growing irritation as he surveyed the disheveled wreck. The brown and green throw cushions were bunched into a corner of the brown and green sofa as though ready for Paul to fall asleep in front of the black television. Shoes, socks and even underwear were scattered in front of the pewter coffee table. Empty soda cans and coffee mugs sat on every flat surface from the fireplace mantel to the floor. His brother needed to spend more time on his housekeeping skills and less time on Anthony's career.

"She's the reason you don't want to be traded, isn't she?" Paul's accusation aggravated Anthony.

What made Jamal and Paul believe that he didn't know his own mind? "No, Paul. *You're* the reason I'm staying in Brooklyn. You're my only living family. Why would I want to move thirteen hundred miles away from you?"

Paul didn't look as though he believed him. "What do you know about this woman?"

Anthony didn't like Paul's tone. "What do you want to know?"

"Can you trust her? Does she have your best interests at heart? You know that I do, but this woman's just using you."

It was *déjà vu* of his conversation with Jamal. "What makes you think that?"

"She's turning you against me." Paul threw up his arms. "You valued my opinion before she made herself a part of your life. Now you're telling me to mind my own business? That's bulls–!"

"I'm not saying you can't give me your opinion." Anthony struggled with feelings of guilt. "When I was growing up, I appreciated your being a father figure in my life. But what I need now is a brother."

"And as your brother, I'm telling you something's up with this woman." Paul planted his hands on his hips. "She's friends with the women who're dating your teammates. You don't think that had something to do with her showing up on your doorstep?"

"Oh, come on, Paul." Anthony turned away. He tried to dismiss his brother's words, but they joined with Jamal's, working their way into his head.

"She wants what they have and she expects you to give it to her. *That's* why she doesn't want you to be traded."

"You're wrong." Anthony turned to leave. As far as he was concerned, Paul could believe whatever he liked. So could Jamal.

But what do I *believe?*

CHAPTER 17

Faith raised her hand in silent greeting to yet another group of coworkers early Monday morning. Just like the first group, they gave her a quizzical look. They all undoubtedly wondered why she kept turning up early just to speak on her cell phone in the lobby of the building where they worked.

It was complicated.

"Lareeta, I've got ten minutes to get to my desk." Faith glanced at her watch. It was almost nine o'clock. "I appreciate your pep talk but could you get to the point. Have more companies rejected the Crew?"

Faith squared her shoulders beneath her white blouse and emerald blazer in preparation for more disappointment. The white and gold tiled lobby smelled like money. Too bad most of the people working in the downtown Brooklyn building didn't make more of it.

"O ye of little faith." Lareeta chuckled as though she never tired of that silly play on Faith's name. "I want you to remember that you're the one who was anxious to jump at our first offer and that I, your ever-wise and experienced agent, urged you to hold on. And. As usual. I was right."

Faith caught her breath. Every muscle in her body tensed. "We've got a better offer?"

A slow pause rolled down the line as though Lareeta was savoring her morning coffee. "A production company has offered for the BKLYN Crew. And wait until you hear their offer."

Lareeta named terms and payments that made Faith gasp again.

"What?" Faith's knees felt weak. In the far corner of the lobby, she collapsed against the wall behind her. The tile was cool against her back even through her thin polyester blouse and linen blazer. "Yes! Yes! A thousand times, yes."

She forced herself to keep her voice low. In her mind, she was jumping up and down, waving her arms, and screaming maniacally.

Am I dreaming?

Lareeta gave a full laugh as though she was being tickled. "I asked you to give us two weeks and in two days we got an offer that changed our luck."

"What do you mean?" Faith remained propped against the wall in the far corner of the lobby. Her body shook with excitement – and disbelief.

Her heart was pounding. With the production company's offer, she'd be able to afford her apartment and other bills without the assistance of roommates. She might even be able to get a place in a nicer part of the borough. Her head was spinning with options.

Was this really happening?

"I leveraged the production company's offer to persuade the publisher to increase its offer." Lareeta paused as though sipping more coffee. She gave a faint, satisfied sigh. "I'm happy to report that they've increased it *significantly*."

Lareeta shared their new proposal with Faith. Faith jerked as though a jolt of electricity shot through her. She'd dreamed of figures like those in her most secret fantasies. She'd never expected to hear them in real life. That's why they're called *fantasies.* But now those dreams were becoming reality. It was almost too much to absorb.

Faith rubbed her forehead. "Should I pinch myself to make sure I'm awake?"

"You're not dreaming, my friend. I believed this would happen for you." Lareeta's voice was happy. In the background, Faith heard a couple of keyboard clicks as though her agent was checking her computer files. "You have talent. It was just a matter of putting you together with the right companies at the right time."

"Thank you for believing in me. This is a great start to the week." Faith glanced at her watch. She had about eight minutes to get to her desk. She felt as though she could fly up the eleven stories. "I hate to cut our conversation short, but I'd better get to work."

"One more thing."

"More good news?"

"That's up to you." Lareeta chuckled. "I mentioned these offers from the production company and the publisher to the Horn. They've requested another comic series from you, if you could come up with something new."

"I've got just the thing." Faith smiled, thinking of the Little Tony comic strip she was developing.

"Good. The Horn's terms are even better than we'd originally asked for with the Crew."

Faith sank farther against the wall. "I can't believe it. I just can't believe it."

"You'd better start believing, my friend. You've got a lot of work to do." Lareeta gave another belly laugh. "And I negotiated all of that in less than two days. Am I good or am I good?"

"You're good."

Lareeta sobered. "I'm sure all of this is overwhelming. We don't have to respond to anyone today. I've forwarded all of the emails with the offers to your personal email account. Take the week, think it over, talk with your mother, then send me an email Friday to let me know what you want to do – or if you need more time."

"Thanks for everything, Lareeta. You're amazing."

"I know." With that characteristically immodest response, her agent ended the call.

Faith glanced at her watch. Six minutes before nine A.M. She'd take the time to risk two more calls. First, she selected Anthony's cell phone number. He should be back from his morning run by now.

She was right. "Tony, hi. Do you have plans for tomorrow night?"

"No." Anthony wasn't his usual welcoming self. He sounded guarded, almost distant. He'd seemed cool when she'd seen him Saturday and Sunday, too.

Had something happened with his contract? "Is everything OK?"

"Yes." Another short almost brusque response.

Should she push him harder? Three straight days of this moodiness was a bit much. Faith injected more enthusiasm into her voice. It was easy enough to do. She had enthusiasm to spare. "I'm calling to ask you to celebrate with me."

"Celebrate what?" His grumpiness was starting to rain on her party of one.

"Are you sure everything's OK? You sound funny. Did something happen?"

"Everything's fine." He must be lying.

Faith let it pass. She was running out of time and she still had one more call to make. "I'll explain everything when I see you tomorrow. I'll be by around seven o'clock. See you then."

She rang off with him before his moodiness did any more damage to her euphoria, then made the call she'd been waiting to make since she was nine years old.

"Hello?"

At the sound of JoyLynn's voice, Faith started to cry. "Mama, we did it."

***

Even Anthony's kiss felt distant. Faith stepped out of his arms Tuesday evening as they stood in the middle of his living room. Concerned, she searched his eyes. What was wrong? She'd come here to share her good news with him. Yesterday, she'd talked at length with her mother, Andrea and Constance. She and her roommates were planning a celebration Wednesday night when they'd all be together. Faith's victory tour wouldn't be complete until she shared her achievement with Anthony. However, it would be selfish to boast of her good news while something obviously continued to plague his mind.

Faith drew him with her to the black leather sofa in his living room. She held his gaze as she tugged him down beside her on the thick cushion. "I've sensed something bothering you for a couple of days now. Every time I ask what's on your mind, you deny that anything's wrong, but I know that's not true. We've only known each other a month, but I wish you'd confide in me. Maybe I can help."

His silent stare was unnerving but Faith forced herself to maintain their eye contact. She wanted to show that she could be strong for both of them.

Finally, he spoke. "What will you do when Andrea and Connie move out of your apartment?"

Faith's eyes widened with surprise. A grateful smile spread her lips. "Is that what's bothering you? You're so sweet, but there's no need to worry. I think I've got everything worked out."

"What're you going to do?"

Faith started to tell him her news, but something in his expression made her hesitate. His features were hard and closed, not in keeping with his caring question. He didn't look like the Anthony she was starting to fall in love with. "Are you certain the only thing on your mind is my living arrangements when Andrea, Connie and Tiff leave?"

Anthony sprang from his sofa with a suddenness that ripped a gasp from her. His bare feet were silent on his blonde wood flooring. She tracked his movements to his sliding glass windows and watched him look out at his view of the tops of the Brooklyn Museum, Botanical Gardens and Prospect Park.

"Why are you with me?" Anthony wouldn't even look at her as he asked the question.

Faith studied the black T-shirt that molded the muscles in his back and the tight blue jeans that did wonderful things to his glutes.

The feelings stirring inside her didn't ward off an uncomfortable chill of foreboding. "What are you implying?"

He looked at her over his shoulder. His beautiful olive eyes were cold and distant. "Why won't you answer?"

"Because it's a very odd question and I want to know what prompted it." Faith clenched her fists in her lap.

Anthony shoved his hands into his pockets and paced back to the sofa. "Is it really just a coincidence that you and your roommates are all dating Monarchs?"

His question stole her breath. Faith stood from the sofa. She was still wearing the copper skirt suit and white blouse she'd worn to work that morning.

"I thought we'd already been through this." Her voice was thin with shock. "My roommates and I aren't groupies."

"I didn't say you were." Anthony rubbed the back of his neck. He paced the length of the sofa and back.

"Then perhaps the term you're looking for is 'opportunists.'"

He jerked his arm between the two of them. "Is this a coincidence or is it something more?"

"You tell me." She was shaking, for pity's sake. "Better yet, ask Troy and Serge, then ask yourself. Who pursued whom? Our getting together was *your* idea, Tony. I'd accepted your apology. *You're* the one who insisted on dinner and a relationship."

And while she was falling in love, he was questioning her integrity.

Anthony came to a stop in front of her. He studied Faith's expression. "Were you hoping I'd ask you to move in with me?"

Who was this monster?

Faith tore her gaze from Anthony and spun on her heels. His suspicions stunned and wounded her. Everything between them – every word, every thought, every feeling – had been a lie. How could she have been such a fool?

She snatched her handbag from his coat closet before confronting him for the last time. He hadn't moved a muscle. That added fuel to the furnace of her temper.

She jerked her purse strap onto her shoulder. "I had reservations about this relationship from the start. I told you that. For your peace of mind, when Andrea, Connie and Tiff move out, don't worry about me. I'll be fine."

CHAPTER 18

"Do you think it's just a coincidence that you, Troy and I are dating women who are roommates?" Anthony followed Serge out of the locker room after practice Wednesday afternoon.

Doubts had plagued him for the past five days, since Friday afternoon when Jamal had planted the seed that Faith was using him. Paul's accusations had bolstered those qualms. Was *she playing me?* The question repeated on a loop in his mind day and night, night and day. The recording had grown even more vicious after Faith had stormed from his condo Tuesday evening.

She'd been shocked and angered by his accusations. Had he made a mistake? The cold finger on the nape of his neck shouted, "*Yes!*"

Serge shrugged his broad shoulders under his navy jersey. His long calves were bared by knee-length khaki shorts. "What else would it be?" The Frenchman's demeanor was dismissive.

Anthony walked with the forward down the hallway of the main floor of the Monarchs' practice facility. The stench of burned popcorn assailed his nostrils. That a teammate didn't bother to read the brief instructions on the bag of vending machine microwave popcorn explained a lot about their horrible practice. They'd finished their ninth day of training camp. They were defending their championship title this season, starting with tomorrow's preseason game in which they were hosting the Boston Celtics in the Empire Arena. But based on today's practice, an observer would think they'd never played basketball together before. In a few days, they'd add Marlon Burress to their roster. How would that work out? Even Warrick Evans disliked the ex-Miami Waves player and Warrick liked everyone.

Anthony pushed aside those worries for now. "Jamal thinks Faith, Andrea and Connie planned our relationships."

"You're listening to *Jamal*?" Serge tossed back his head and laughed. "That's a good one."

"I'm serious." Anthony's gaze wavered. It sounded stupid when Serge said it out loud.

Serge suddenly stopped. His large hand shot out to catch Anthony's right upper arm. The weight of his black nylon gym bag and Serge's hand held him in place.

"You're listening to *Jamal*?" This time, his dark blue eyes were wide with horror.

"It's not just Jamal. My brother made some comments, too."

"I don't know your brother, but I have to wonder about you if you're giving credence to something said by someone who calls *himself* Jam-On-It." Serge shamed him with a look. He released Anthony's arm.

"I know. I shouldn't have listened to him." Anthony couldn't hold Serge's gaze.

Serge must have heard the wealth of frustration in his voice. "What have you done?"

The sleepless night, morning workout and four-hour practice under DeMarcus's pitiless direction were taking a toll on him. Anthony wanted to get home and fall into bed, but he wouldn't be able to sleep until he confessed his latest sin.

He turned to continue down the main hallway to the practice facility's front exit. Serge fell into step beside him. They walked past the recreation area with its pool table, ping pong table and television; the vending machines, which stood beside the still smoking microwave oven; and the empty lounge.

Anthony felt Serge staring at his profile as he waited for a response. He greeted the security guards, then pushed through the glass front door. "I asked Faith if she was hoping I'd ask her to move in with me once Andrea and Connie moved out of their apartment."

Serge's hand on Anthony's upper arm again hampered his progress. "You must be insane."

"Saying it out loud to you, it sounds insane." Anthony looked around the Monarchs' grounds. The breeze off the marina was a little bit colder this afternoon. The sky was a little grayer.

"When did your asinine performance occur?"

"Last night." Anthony sighed but the pain in his chest didn't ease.

Serge dropped his hand from Anthony's arm. His blue eyes burned with anger. "That's the second time you've insulted my friend."

"Worse, I insulted someone I've come to care for. A lot." His admission seemed to diffuse some of Serge's wrath.

"Tony, *mon ami*, you're an idiot for listening to Jamal." Serge headed toward the parking lot.

"I know." Anthony fell into step beside his teammate. He should have spoken with Serge first.

"You're an even bigger idiot for thinking Faith was using you." The Frenchman adjusted the strap of the black and silver nylon gym bag on his shoulder. "Last night, Faith probably planned to tell you about the contracts she was offered for her comic strips. Trust me, she won't need help with her rent."

Anthony gaped at the other man. "A publisher made an offer for her comic strips?"

Serge nodded. "And a production company. Faith can take care of herself."

Anthony's face burned with shame. That's what Faith had said as she'd stormed from his condo – and presumably his life – last night. Even before that, she'd asked him to help her celebrate.

I'm an idiot!

"What am I going to do?" Anthony broke the uneasy silence. His gym bag slipped down his right shoulder as he scrubbed his face with his hands.

"Crawl to her on your hands and knees, and beg for forgiveness." Serge sounded serious. He stepped into the parking lot and started weaving in and out of the lanes of cars.

"Do you think it would work?" Anthony was willing to try anything for a third chance with Faith.

"If I were Faith, no. But it's a start." Serge stopped beside his silver Mercedes Benz and deactivated the alarm. He opened the driver's side door and tossed his gym bag onto the passenger's seat. "Good luck."

Anthony watched his teammate pull away before turning to find his Lexus. When he and Faith first met, she'd made him apologize twice before she forgave him.

How many chances of forgiveness do I have left?

CHAPTER 19

Anthony crossed his fingers before answering the security intercom near the front door of his condo later Wednesday evening. *Please let it be Faith. Please. Please.* "Chambers."

"Mister Chambers." Leon the doorman took his job very seriously. "Your brother's here to see you. Should I send him up?"

After their last exchange, Anthony was tempted to say no. "Yes, please, Leon. Thank you."

He released the intercom, then wandered away from his front door. It would take Paul a few minutes to get to Anthony's eleventh floor residence. It was nearly seven o'clock Wednesday evening. He still hadn't heard from Faith.

Anthony stopped before the large, picture window in his living room and stared toward the Brooklyn Museum, the Brooklyn Botanical Gardens and the tree tops marking Prospect Park. Faith hadn't returned any of his messages, not the one he'd left on her work phone nor the three he'd recorded on her cell phone. She hadn't responded to his text messages, either. Had she run out of grace? Even if she didn't forgive him, he wanted the opportunity to apologize for hurting her.

The knock on his front door reminded him that he'd been waiting for his brother. Anthony checked his cell phone again before walking barefoot across his cool blonde wood flooring. He glanced through the security peephole. Paul stood on the other side. He didn't look pleased. Anthony opened the door anyway, stepping back to let him in.

"I'm your brother." Paul crossed the threshold into the condo's entryway. He pushed the side of Anthony's head with the first two fingers of his right hand before walking on. "Why do I have to be *announced* before I can be *allowed* upstairs?"

"It's called security." Anthony closed and locked his door before leading his brother into his living room. "I didn't expect to see you so soon after our argument Thursday. It hasn't even been a week. Your sulks usually last a lot longer."

Paul glared at him. "I don't sulk."

"Yes, you do." Anthony stopped in front of his fireplace. He checked his cell phone again. Still no response from Faith. She spent Wednesday evenings with her roommates, though.

Is that the reason she's not calling me back?

"Jeez, this place is really clean." Paul's voice carried from behind him. "Mom would be proud."

Anthony shifted his gaze to his brother. "Why're you here?" Obviously not to apologize.

"Nyles said you fired him last week." Paul's announcement was a mixture of shock and confusion.

"Why did you call my former agent?" Hadn't they just talked about this?

"*He* called *me*."

Perfect. Anthony rubbed the muscles knotting at the base of his neck. His cell phone still hadn't vibrated or chimed. "He was damaging my relationship with the Monarchs."

Paul crossed the living room and settled on the edge of Anthony's armchair. "Listen, what you said Thursday about me trying to live your life really bothered me–"

"I'm sorry–"

"No, it bothered me because you're right." Paul braced his elbows on his thighs and cradled his forehead. "I introduced you to the game, but it was your hard work and talent that got you that ring."

"A smart owner, skilled coaching and talented teammates helped."

"Yeah." Paul flashed a grin that didn't last. He stood and offered Anthony his right hand. "I wanted to tell you that you're right. I'll stop trying to be your surrogate father and just be your brother instead."

Anthony stepped away from his fireplace and pulled his brother into an embrace. "Thanks, man."

Paul stepped back. "Can I ask you something – as your brother?"

Anthony searched Paul's features, letting his arms drop. "You want to know about Faith."

"You've only known her a month." Paul held his gaze. "How do you know you can trust her?"

"If it wasn't for Faith, you and I wouldn't be talking like this. She gave me the courage to tell you how I feel."

Paul was silent for several seconds as he seemed to process Anthony's words. "She put you in touch with your feelings?"

Anthony gave him a sheepish grin. "I know it sounds stupid."

"It sounds like what you needed."

"How do I convince *her* of that?"

Paul patted his shoulder and gave him an empathetic look. "It's not about convincing her that you need her. She knows that. You need to convince her that she wants you."

Anthony massaged his neck, glancing at the phone he still held in his hand. "And how do I do that?"

Paul spread his arms. "Your guess is as good as mine, little brother."

"That was less than helpful." He needed a plan, some kind of inspiration. And Faith.

CHAPTER 20

Anthony studied Faith standing at the edge of the Monarchs' practice court closest to the exit doors. Her citrus orange sheath dress skimmed her slender, toned figure. It ended just below her knees, showing off her long, toned calves. Her lavender tote bag swung from her right shoulder.

He took a deep breath as he walked away from the locker room doors. The court smelled of lemon floor wax and honest sweat. His sneakers squeaked against the high-gloss hardwood. The noise drew Faith's attention away from her cell phone. The welcoming expression forming on her pixie features winked away.

He deserved that. Still Anthony struggled not to let his shoulders roll forward in defeat. "Thanks for coming."

She looked confused. "I'm here to see Serge."

"I asked him to call you because you wouldn't return any of my messages."

"I don't need to hear anything else from you." Faith took a step back, increasing the space between them to more than an arm's length. But she didn't walk away. Small victory.

"I'm sorry, Faith." Anthony held her gaze. He fisted his hands to resist the urge to reach for her. "I never should've doubted your intent with our relationship. I know you too well, and I owe you better."

"Then why did you?" She sounded more curious than convinced.

"I'm a fool."

"That's not much of an answer."

Anthony spread his arms. "It's the only one I have."

Faith was silent as she searched his face. Anthony stared back. It had been a long four days since he'd seen her. He drank in the features he'd missed so much: her wide chocolate brown eyes, full candy pink lips, and delicate cinnamon cheekbones.

"You won't get an argument from me." Faith turned toward the practice court's exit.

"Wait." Anthony caught her arm with reflexes honed for an NBA championship. He'd never appreciated them more. "Can you forgive me?" He released her.

"I can forgive you, but I can't forget." Faith turned on him. "You hurt me."

Her voice was raw emotion: sorrow, anger, confusion, regret. It echoed around the court, damning him with the truth.

Anthony felt her pain as his own. "I'm so sorry, Faith."

"That's the second time you've doubted my integrity." She dug her index finger into his chest, driving him back. "What happened to 'judge not that ye shall not be judged'?"

"I was wrong." Anthony didn't shield himself from her attack, physical or verbal. "'For there is not a just man upon earth that doeth good and sinneth not.'" Quoting Ecclesiastes, chapter seven, verse twenty was a desperate play, but he sensed he was reaching her.

Faith took a deeper breath and drilled her finger into his chest again. "I thought things would be different when we got to know each other."

"They were."

"It's only been a month but we talked on the phone every day and saw each other several times a week. I thought we'd connected. Dreamers have to stick together and all that stuff. But maybe I wasn't dreaming. Maybe I was just asleep."

"You're wrong." Anthony took hold of her hand, pressing her palm to his chest. "I was the one asleep at the wheel. I listened to other people, thinking they had my back when I should've followed my instincts. You woke me before I went over a cliff."

Faith wrenched her hand from his hold. "Who're you listening to now?"

"Myself." Anthony held her gaze, willing her to believe in him. "I know what I need in my life."

"You've had a great awakening." Faith circled him, giving him a scoffing once over. "What is it you think you need?"

Anthony met her mocking gaze over his shoulder. "You."

Faith's chocolate eyes widened in surprise, then narrowed in challenge. "Words, Tony. Very pretty words, but actions speak louder."

He turned to face her. "Then give me the chance to show you that I mean what I say." He spread his arms to encompass the practice court. "Give us a chance to start over where we began."

Faith crossed her arms. "And you'll put your words to deeds?"

She was softening toward him. It was in the easing of the tension around her lips and the hope dawning in her eyes.

Anthony took a chance and tugged her arms free. He drew her into his embrace and whispered against her lips. "That's my game plan."

"Good." She slid her hands over his chest and wrapped her arms around his neck. "But if you mess up this time, I'm benching you."

Thank you for reading *Game Plan*. I hope you enjoyed Anthony and Faith's, and Serge and Constance's stories. If you did, please help other readers find *Game Plan*:

1. This book is lendable, so send it to a friend who you think might like it so she can discover me, too.
2. Help other people find this book by writing a review.
3. Subscribe to my enewsletter to find out about my upcoming releases.
4. Like my Facebook page: www.facebook.com/patricia.sargeant.9

About the Author

Award-winning author Patricia Sargeant writes romantic suspense, contemporary romance, paranormals, epic fantasies and time travels. She writes cozy mysteries under the pseudonym Olivia Matthews. She also wrote contemporary romance under her Regina Hart pseudonym. For more information about Patricia, her books and her pseudonyms, please visit her web site, PatriciaSargeant.com.

You also can friend her on Facebook and follow her on Twitter. Her email address is BooksByPatricia@yahoo.com.

Other Books by Patricia Sargeant / Regina Hart / Olivia Matthews

Patricia Sargeant's titles

You Belong to Me

On Fire

Sweet Deception

Heated Rivalry

Brooklyn Monarchs series (written as Regina Hart)

Fast Break

Smooth Play

Keeping Score

Brooklyn Monarchs series (written as Patricia Sargeant)

Game Plan

Game Time Decision *(coming 2018)*

Finding Home series (written as Regina Hart)

Trinity Falls

Harmony Cabins

Wishing Lake

Mystic Park

A Christmas Kiss *(anthology)*

Anderson Family (written as Regina Hart)

The Love Game

Passion Play

Sister Lou mysteries (written as Olivia Matthews)

Mayhem & Mass *(available December 2017)*

Peril & Prayer *(coming 2018)*

Made in the USA
Columbia, SC
27 January 2023

10344715R00100